American History Through People Who Looked to The LORD

MARGARET WHITAKER

InspiringVoices®
A Service of Guideposts

Inspiring Voices books may be ordered through booksellers or by contacting:

Inspiring Voices
1663 Liberty Drive
Bloomington, IN 47403
www.inspiringvoices.com
1-(866) 697-5313

Because of the dynamic nature of the Internet, any web addresses or links contained in this book may have changed since publication and may no longer be valid. The views expressed in this work are solely those of the author and do not necessarily reflect the views of the publisher, and the publisher hereby disclaims any responsibility for them.

Certain stock imagery © Thinkstock.
Any people depicted in stock imagery provided by Thinkstock are models,
and such images are being used for illustrative purposes only.

Scriptures taken from The Holy Bible, 21st Century King James version CKJ21®,
Copyright © 1994, Deuel Enterprises, Inc., Gary SD 57237, and used by permission.

ISBN: 978-1-4624-0017-1 (e)
ISBN: 978-1-4624-0018-8 (sc)

Library of Congress Control Number: 2011939147

Printed in the United States of America

Inspiring Voices rev. date: 10/24/2011

Contents

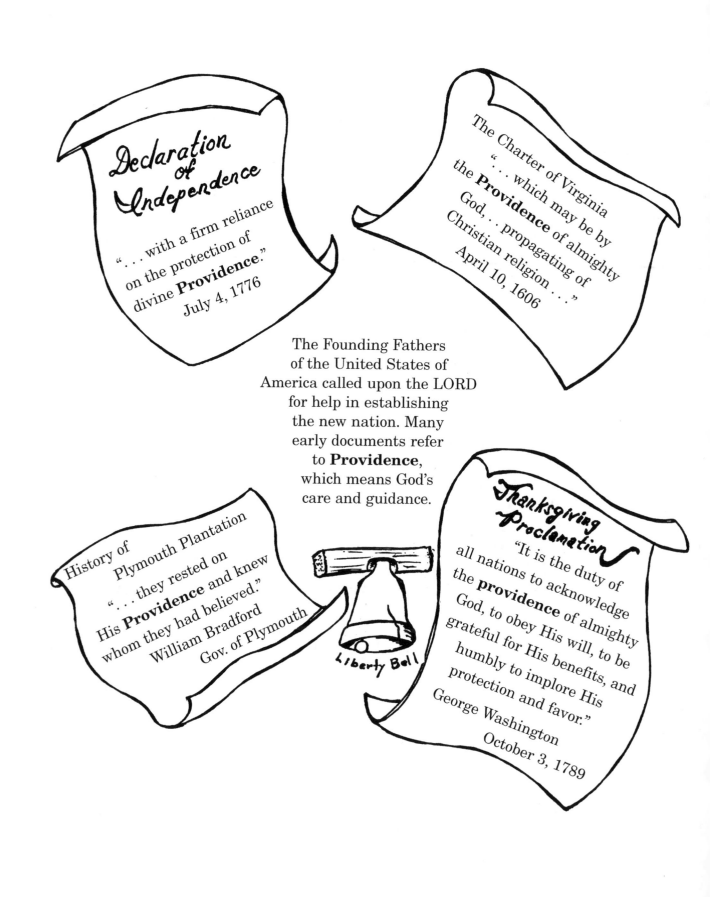

Declaration of Independence

"... with a firm reliance on the protection of divine **Providence**."
July 4, 1776

The Charter of Virginia

"... which may be by the **Providence** of almighty God, ... propagating of Christian religion ..."
April 10, 1606

The Founding Fathers of the United States of America called upon the LORD for help in establishing the new nation. Many early documents refer to **Providence**, which means God's care and guidance.

History of Plymouth Plantation

"... they rested on His **Providence** and knew whom they had believed."
William Bradford
Gov. of Plymouth

Liberty Bell

Thanksgiving Proclamation

"It is the duty of all nations to acknowledge the **providence** of almighty God, to obey His will, to be grateful for His benefits, and humbly to implore His protection and favor."
George Washington
October 3, 1789

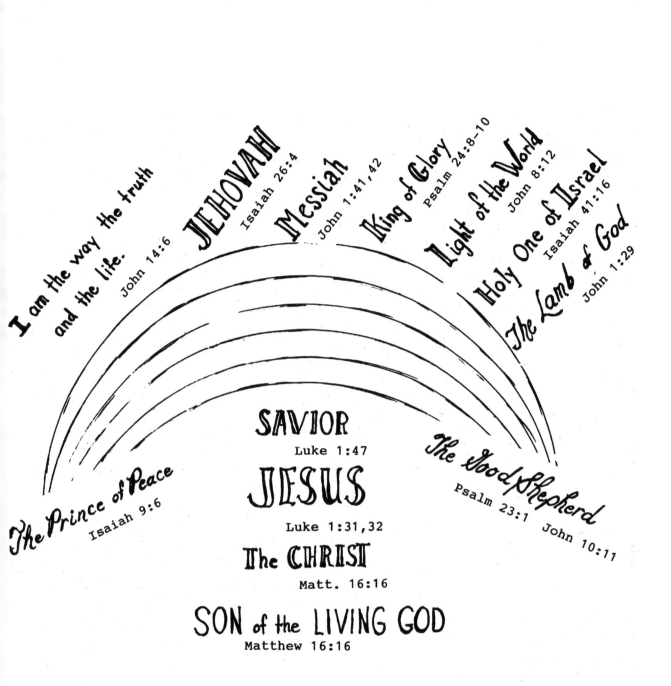

I am the way the truth and the life. John 14:6

JEHOVAH Isaiah 26:4

Messiah John 1:41,42

King of Glory Psalm 24:8-10

Light of the World John 8:12

Holy One of Israel Isaiah 41:16

The Lamb of God John 1:29

SAVIOR
Luke 1:47

JESUS
Luke 1:31,32

The CHRIST
Matt. 16:16

SON of the LIVING GOD
Matthew 16:16

The Good Shepherd Psalm 23:1 John 10:11

The Prince of Peace Isaiah 9:6

Find three more names of the LORD in the Bible.

1. _____

2. _____

3. _____

You may choose one and make a name plaque.

You can color the rainbow above and other pictures in this book.   Gen. 9:11-13

(Colored pencil, then marker over it does not soak through so much. Crayons work well.)

UNIT 1   CHOOSE A NAME

Choose the name of a character(s) in American history. Begin to read books about that person. Keep a record of what you read—title, author, and location of the book, so you can find it again easily. Look for an episode in that person's life that you think would make a good story.

WRITE A STORY

During the year you will work on a historical fiction story(ies) based on fact but including conversations and ideas from your imagination. As you progress through the book, read the CREATIVE WRITING sections. Make additions or changes in your story(ies) so you can check each square or draw the pen in the inkwell. To be a writer means to be a rewriter. Ask your teacher for help.

A good story needs a conflict that your main character has to overcome. Try to introduce the conflict early in your story. Add more and more difficulties to increase suspense, until the height of the story, when your character solves the problem.

Bring in as many senses as you can: sights, sounds, scents, colors, and textures to make it more believable. Intersperse the main character's feelings with the action. Remember, it is through his or her eyes. Draw and color a picture to illustrate it.

WRITE A PLAY

You may prefer to write a play about the person you choose. Research what daily life was like at the time of your play, so scenes will be more realistic.

ASK A GRANDPARENT

You could ask a grandparent, or other relative, about a major event in history that he or she lived through. How did it affect his or her life?

If you would like to write a story or play about an ancestor, BE SURE to GET WRITTEN PERMISSION from the related parent.

The stories that follow are about people who actually lived. I found their names by researching my family tree. The characters became involved in events during their time and sometimes helped history turn out the way it did. It is my hope that by reading the fictionalized stories, you will feel a part of events through their eyes and emotions. Historical notes after each story tell which parts are true. By choosing names in American history to research, you will, I am sure, find many interesting true stories.

author

Native Americans
Underground Railroad agents
Puritans
whaling men
English
Presbyterians
farmers
Quakers
Dutch
abolitionists
pioneers
merchants
Baptists

"But as for me and my house, we will serve the LORD."
Josh. 24:15b

3

**"Show me Thy ways, O LORD;
teach me Thy paths."**
Psalm 25:4

UNIT 2   **POCAHONTAS RENAMED REBECCA**

"Here I am! It's me, Pocahontas!" Pocahontas leaned her head out a window of the 'giant dugout'. She waved. "Wait for me!" Her long black braids dropped out over the edge of the ship.

Why did her friends race away with that golden pot? Pocahontas dashed to the other side of the room and pushed on the door. It held fast. "Why did they bring me here to look at the 'dugout'," she thought, "and leave me here in the captain's cabin?"

"Capt'n! Capt'n," Pocahontas called. No one answered. Pocahontas put her ear against the floor. Footsteps tapped in the distance. The walls began to creak and the ceiling shuddered.

From the window, Pocahontas blinked as the shore began to move. Her heart tightened. Her friends had vanished. The wigwams of her aunt's village became smaller until she could see them no more.

Pocahontas began to cry. Then, raising her chin, she said, "I must not cry. The daughter of a great chief does not weep."

A flock of seagulls swooped down from above and glided in the air. "Sister

4

Seagull! Go tell Wahunsonacawh, my father, I am here, caught in the giant dugout with the Englishmen. He will send help!"

The birds hovered a moment and were gone. Pocahontas sighed with relief. "Now my father will send his braves to rescue me."

Happily, she set about to search the captain's cabin. In one corner she found a large trunk. It glowed like a fresh brown chestnut. She had never felt wood so smooth. Slowly she raised its lid.

She lifted a tool and peeked through. How big everything became! It startled her. The heavy lid slipped and banged shut.

Suddenly an angry, oversized, green eye stared at her! The telescope fell from her hand. Glass splintered at her feet.

"Pocahontas! You must behave!" The English captain glowered at her. She backed up against the wall. "You will be our captive until your father, Chief Wahunsonacawh, returns our men and muskets."

Pocahontas felt as if the cabin closed in on her. She could not breathe. Pocahontas knew her father would not bow easily to his enemies.

"We will take you to Henrico, near Jamestown," were the captain's final words.

In Henrico, Pocahontas stared at the plain white walls of the parsonage. She thought about her wigwam walls of grass. She missed their warm tan hue and pungent scent.

"Pocahontas, listen!" frowned Reverend Whitaker, "A, B, C." He pointed to an a,b,c,darius at the front of the room.

"Why must I learn to read?" thought Pocahontas. "I need no strange marks to grow corn and beans."

She glanced at the ceiling. No bunches of dried corn hung overhead as in her wigwam. She thought of all the baskets of food she had brought with her sisters to the English during their Starving Time. She had warned John Smith of danger many times. He had been grateful, but where was her friend now?

"Is this how the English honor me? They trap me?" She had seen the forts and high walls on her way in. Soldiers roamed everywhere. Had Sister Seagull told her father?

5

Pocahontas breathed a deep sigh. "Oh!" The new garments given her by the ladies of Jamestown pinched. "It's as if my aunt made me a birch bark dress," she imagined. She missed her soft deerskin.

Days went by. Reverend Whitaker repeated the unfamiliar sounds. Pocahontas was no closer to reading, and the chief no closer to delivering the Englishmen with their muskets. Every evening she sat in a stiff pew at church. Where was her father to take her away from this hard, uncomfortable place? She wanted to run free again in the forest, to feel the brook bubbling through her fingers and the cool moss under her feet. But her father did not come.

One day during her lesson came a knock at the door. A young Englishman ducked as he entered. He held a pile of plants that were spotty and wilted.

"Reverend, something must be done!" declared the visitor. He looked in Pocahontas's direction and smiled. He spoke to the reverend: "Our crops are dying."

"I can help! I grow good corn!" Pocahontas jumped to her feet.

"You are now an English lady," emphasized the reverend. "You must learn to read."

"You need corn to live!" replied Pocahontas.

"Your lovely student speaks the truth, Reverend," answered John Rolfe.

"Very well, Pocahontas, you may show John how to grow corn. Your lesson is over for today."

Pocahontas showed John how to mound the soil for plants to breathe. She planted corn, beans, and squash. "Now Three Sisters will help each other. The beans will lean on the cornstalk and the squash will give its shade."

"You are clever, Pocahontas," smiled John.

"My people know this." A tear fell from her eye. "They were my people. Now they do not come for me."

In the days that followed, Pocahontas and John cared for their corn plants. They grew to care for each other even more. John helped Pocahontas learn to read. The hard times of the past melted away. She no longer felt like a captive. Soon they were to be married. The colonists were delighted, and her father sent his blessing.

Pocahontas glanced out the church window and looked wistfully up the river. Maybe her father would come for her naming and wedding ceremonies?

Colonists in their colorful best arrived from Jamestown. Braves in feathered regalia came from her Powhatan people upriver. Women of the tribe brought baskets filled with wildflowers. They hung the baskets and set a daisy arch as a doorway to the aisle; the perfume of blossoms filling the air.

Pocahontas asked her uncle, "Will Father come for my wedding?"

7

"Your father will never set his feet in the English village, but he sends you this chain of pearls." Her uncle fastened them around Pocahontas's neck. Now Pocahontas knew her father remembered and loved her.

English and Native Americans soon crowded into the small building. Could enemies sit together? The hymn singing began.

It was time! Pocahontas took her uncle's arm as they passed through the arch. She wore a plain, white muslin gown. The full skirt with petticoats rustled like fallen leaves before the frost. She held a trailing bunch of pink and blue morning glories.

"For in Thee do I trust," the congregation sang. "Help me to know the path that I must walk."

Between words of the song Pocahontas heard delicate footsteps behind her. She turned and saw the young fawn that followed her. An arm from a pew reached out to stop it.

"Let him stay. He is my brother Fawn," she whispered. "He has come for my wedding." The fawn nuzzled her. With her uncle and brother, Pocahontas made her stately way down the flowered aisle.

There at the altar, waiting to greet her, stood John, strong, yet gentle. She smiled at him and he took her hand.

"Pocahontas," began Reverend Whitaker, "Matoaka, daughter of Wahunsonacawh, chief of many tribes, I baptize you Rebecca. You are as Rebecca in the Good Book. Two nations in her were joined. From this day forward, you shall be known only by the name Rebecca."

Though she knew she would be called Rebecca, in her heart she would remain Pocahontas.

The ladies of Jamestown brought a magnificent dresscoat of the finest brocade, trimmed with ruffled white silk and gold threads. They helped her on with it for the wedding.

"John, do you take Rebecca to be your wife?" Reverend Whitaker turned to Mr. Rolfe, "to honor in times of health and times of sickness?"

John answered, "I do."

"Rebecca, do you take John to be your husband, to love in times of plenty and times of famine?" asked the minister.

"I do," she responded. Pocahontas felt content.

"May we now have peace," declared the minister. "Let it be called the Peace of Pocahontas."

Bells rang out.

NAMES

Pocahontas
The name given by her father means "playful one."

Matoaka
Her secret name, known only to her tribesmen, means "Little Snow Feather." In the winter she wore a long mantle of white swan feathers.

Non-pareil
The name given to Pocahontas by John Smith means "there is no one parallel or like her."

HISTORY

The story of Pocahontas saving John Smith's life is well known. John Smith himself wrote about it in his account of Jamestown Colony, settled by the English in 1607. It was sometimes a custom that a Powhatan Native American woman could make a gesture of saving an enemy's life. That enemy would be inducted and obligated to the tribe. Chief Wahunsonacawh wanted weapons from John Smith and so could have staged this "rescue." Pocahontas was then Smith's guardian. She did warn John Smith of danger several times. In 1609 Smith returned to England because of an injury.

John Smith

Fighting broke out between the English at Jamestown and Native Americans, and in 1612 Captain Argall took Pocahontas prisoner. With a copper kettle, he bribed someone to get Pocahontas onto the ship. According to the secretary of the colony then, she was "taken weeping" to Jamestown. She would be a hostage for Englishmen and weapons in Powhatan's possession.

Pocahontas was taken to Henrico, a small, heavily fortified town and instructed by Reverend Whitaker in Christianity and reading. Reverend Whitaker said of Native Americans, that they have reasonable souls and intellectual capacities as well as we do; we all have Adam for our common ancestor. At eighteen, while still in Henrico, Pocahontas met John Rolfe, a planter. He helped her learn to read English.

Her father did not return all the weapons and so Pocahontas remained a prisoner. According to the colony's secretary, Pocahontas said that if her father had loved her, he would not think she was less valuable than old swords and muskets, so she would dwell with the Englishmen, who loved her.

*"Again, the Kingdom of Heaven is like unto
a merchant man, seeking goodly pearls,
who, when he had found one pearl
of great price, went and sold all
that he had and bought it."* Matt. 13: 45, 46

Reverend Whitaker renamed Pocahontas to be "Rebecca" and baptized her. He and/or John Rolfe's minister performed the wedding ceremony. Pocahontas did wear a pearl necklace that her father had sent with her uncle for the wedding. She and John had a son, Thomas, and lived for a short while near Henrico. So began the Peace of Pocahontas, which lasted several years.

In 1616, Pocahontas, John, and Thomas traveled with several tribesmen and women to England to help promote the Virginia colony. The chief of the Powhatans had given Tomocomo, one of the group, a stick and told him to count all the English he saw by making notches. Tomocomo soon gave up the idea because there were so many, and he threw away the stick. Meanwhile, John Smith wrote to Queen Anne about Pocahontas to introduce her to the court. He wrote that Pocahontas was the one person above all others who helped save Jamestown Colony from starvation. Pocahontas attended royal parties where she charmed King James and Queen Anne with her poise. John Smith surprised Pocahontas with a visit, for she thought he had died. Pocahontas said to him that she would always be his countryman.

Pocahontas

The Rolfes were on their way back to Virginia, but Pocahontas became ill, probably with a lung infection due to London smog. She died at twenty-two and is buried in Gravesend, England. On the site is a plaque honoring "Princess Pocahontas . . . Gentle and humane, she was the friend of the earliest struggling English colonists whom she nobly rescued, protected, and helped." John returned to Virginia, while Thomas grew up in England. Thomas traveled to Virginia later and raised a family. Many descendants of Pocahontas live throughout America, especially in the Southeast. Some families of Blairs, Bolings, Lewises, and Randolphs are among her progeny.

Creative Writing

Check here if you did this in your story.

(tips from the author)

SHOW your main character's traits through the action. I wanted to show that, as a Native American, Pocahontas believed in communicating with animals, so I put in Sister Seagull for Pocahontas to ask for help. Pocahontas seems to have been curious about the newcomers in her land, so I had her investigate the captain's sea chest. Most of all, I wanted to show that Pocahontas was kind and gentle. I put in a fawn to follow her into her wedding. First I thought of the fawn munching on her bridal bouquet, but that would just show he liked to eat flowers. I wanted to show that a gentle animal liked Pocahontas's gentle spirit.

Circle or underline parts of the story that show what Pocahontas was like. Then write about something you think Pocahontas might do that would show one of her traits.

_____

_____

_____

_____

_____

WORD STUDY

Use clues from the story to fill in the puzzle. (Puzzle words: abcdarius, descendant, glowered, hovered, mantle, muslin, poised, progeny, pungent, and urgent)

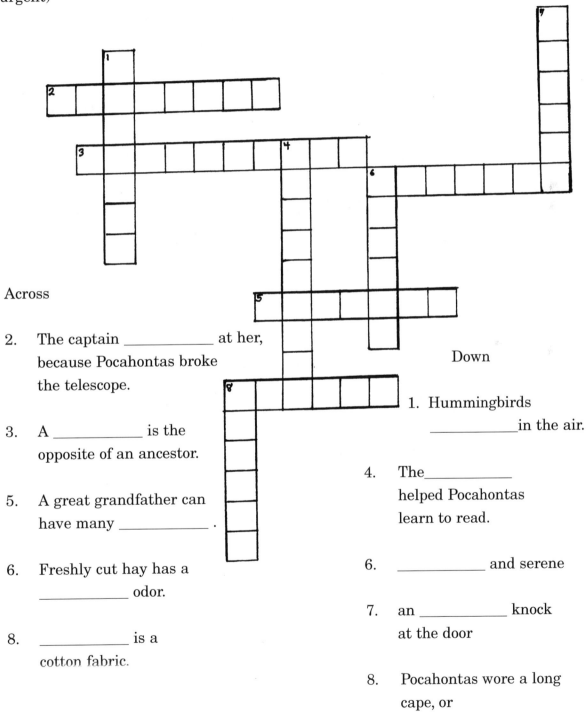

Across

2. The captain _____ at her, because Pocahontas broke the telescope.

3. A _____ is the opposite of an ancestor.

5. A great grandfather can have many _____ .

6. Freshly cut hay has a _____ odor.

8. _____ is a cotton fabric.

Down

1. Hummingbirds _____ in the air.

4. The_____ helped Pocahontas learn to read.

6. _____ and serene

7. an _____ knock at the door

8. Pocahontas wore a long cape, or

QUESTIONS TO DISCUSS

1. What did the wooden stake that Tomocomo took to England show about the

    differences between the English and Native American cultures? Advantages?

    Disadvantages?

2. Why do you think the English were pleased for Pocahontas and John Rolfe to

    be getting married? And why do you think Wahunsonacawh gave his blessing?

3. Why do you think Wahunsonacawh, sometimes called Powhatan, would not set
    foot in the English village?

    Do you think he wanted to come to Pocahontas's wedding?

4. How can God direct you on the path He wants you to go? Let's PRAY:

    (You can write your prayers on a **separate sheet of paper to keep**

    private, or say them silently, if you wish.) _____

    _____

    _____

    _____

    _____

*"And He said unto them,
Go ye into all the world,
and preach the Gospel
to every creature."*
Mark 16: 15

UNIT 3

HANG ON!

The ceiling shook. Crack! Sawdust filtered onto the women's white caps and upturned faces, their eyes wide with fright. Crying children hugged their mothers. The *Mayflower* rolled again. Timbers rattled. The floor sloshed.

"Quick, Damaris!" Mrs. Hopkins hurried her little girl. Women with children scattered into the dim corners.

John Howland looked up from the trunk he had carefully lashed to a pillar. The mighty beam above hung at a precarious slant. Sailors and Pilgrims rushed about the crowded cabin.

"This beam must be raised at once or the next wave could bring the deck down upon us!" Bradford called out. "Get the jack!"

John and several other young men, using winches, raised the heavy iron jack out of the ship's hold and edged it up under the crack in the ceiling.

"We must straighten the broken main beam to hold all the others in place," directed Captain Jones.

John took one arm of the jack and William Bradford the other. They pushed in opposite directions to twist the jack upward. John felt his wet woolen socks up to his baggy knickers. He shivered. His short, woolen jacket was soaked with sea water. His curly, copper colored beard dripped. John slipped in a puddle and William lost his grip.

John slumped over the arm of the jack. Would he ever get to the New World? He thought about the Old World. For him it meant London—smog, crowded alleys, his brother's draper shop, and tailoring that bored him. He wanted adventure! Adventure in the big new country. He knew he was strong and could help build it. He had not been able to pay for his

15

trip, so he had indentured himself as Mr. Carver's servant. After seven years he would be free. But would his adventure end here on the ocean?

"Block and tackle, mate!" It was Captain Jones. "And plenty of rope!"

All eyes fastened on the beam above. Not a voice could be heard. The group waited. They heard only the waves slamming into the ship, timbers groaning, and sloshing sounds with every roll.

Sailors rushed in, loaded with pulleys and coils of rope. In minutes they knotted a pulley to each arm of the jack and stretched the ropes around the closest pillars.

John took the end of a rope and anchored himself to another post. William did the same.

"Heave! Heave!" commanded the captain. The heavy iron plate at the top of the jack inched its way up to the broken beam. John and William strained at the ropes. Slowly, slowly . . . done!

John fell back with a sigh of relief onto his trunk and leaned against the post. The group sat quiet again, stunned at their close call.

"LET US TURN BACK!" came a loud voice out of the group.

"I say we should have accepted Captain John Smith's offer to come with us. He helped establish a successful colony in Jamestown," said Mr. Hopkins.

"I am cold and tired of this voyage. I just want to go home to Leyden," grumbled Giles. "I wish I were on the canal fishing for eels."

"There are many fish in the New World," said his father. "So many codfish you can scoop them up with a ladle."

"If the sea does not swallow you first!" Deacon Carver steadied himself.

"We want a healthy life for our children in the New World."

"Well, they may not be so healthy if they meet natives in the New World! I am for turning back."

The *Mayflower* took another roll. All the Pilgrims held tightly to their belongings.

The children cried, except little Henry, who, clutching his stool, slid across the floor and squealed with delight. A few Pilgrims laughed.

"I picked a worm out of my biscuit this morning." Young Elizabeth puckered her face. "And the drink gets greener every day. I want to go back to Leyden."

"Let's go back!" chimed Priscilla Mullens.

"You grew weary from shuttling your loom all day," answered her mother.

"In Holland the floor did not sway under my loom like this cabin gone crazy."

"War might break out again between Spain and Holland." Mr. Tilley raised an eyebrow of concern. "Besides, we want you to speak English— 'Good morning,' not 'Goed morgen.' "

"If we survive this storm, I am for turning back to England," a Londoner added. "There we had no storms like this!"

"There we had the king's men hunting our dear Reverend Brewster at every turn!" William Bradford looked at his good friend and mentor.

"Well, if he gave up printing those pamphlets against the Church of England, maybe King James would have left him alone!" retorted the Londoner.

"Never give up printing the word against tyranny!" said Reverend Brewster, glancing up at the beam.

"Aye! Aye!" echoed some of the men.

"I do NOT want to go back to England because my poor friend was put in jail for stealing a potato," said Giles, fighting back the tears. "Remember Father?"

"Yes, I do remember, Giles, and the lord of the manor's son had no punishment for stealing a golden goblet!" He patted Giles shoulder gently.

John thought about all of this.

The ocean roared outside. It seeped through the *Mayflower* with every roll, popping bits of oakum and raining on the Pilgrims.

 "Remember our homes were watched day and night in England," said William Bradford. "We could not move about for fear a spy would report us. We had to move our meetings to a new house each week. In the New World we will be able to gather together as we please." He looked at each one with affection.

A sailor elbowed into the little group. "You Pilgrims with your sponge bucket *Speedwell*! We lost two good months trying to fix that old wreck. Now it is November—no time to cross the North Atlantic!"

At that, John sprang off his chest, climbed up the ladder above the grating, and braced himself against the storm. He clung to the mast as the ship teetered below him. The huge canvas flapped with every gust. Sailors perched among the ropes while the sea snatched at them. The mast groaned. Would it hold?

John edged along the side of the ship. The wind whipped his face.

"Get below, pilgrim!" bellowed a seaman.

John turned to glance over his shoulder. The green-grey sea, menacing, rose higher and higher behind him. The *Mayflower* lurched. The deck fell away beneath his feet.

Slam! A mighty rush swept him off! Where was the deck? Cold bubbles crashed over him. Salty foam filled his mouth.

"Hold your breath!" John told himself. "Find the top!" Had the sailors seen him wash overboard? "Even if the Pilgrims tell Captain Jones I have not returned, it will be too late. Besides, they are arguing. How long will it be before they think of me?"

John felt himself sink. His legs ached with cold. He was turning numb. His lungs filled to bursting. "Oh help me!" He thought of the words he had heard the Pilgrims sing, "The Lord came down to rescue me from great waves that . . . might . . ."

With all his strength he kicked and thrust his arms up. There . . . a rope! He grasped it! "HANG ON!" John told himself.

A blurry, watery figure leaning down towards him became larger and larger. Many hands pulled him up out of the angry sea. John gasped and sputtered. There he was on his hands and knees, catching his breath. John thought how he had sunk to the depths and been preserved. "Now I know. Whatever the others decide, MY vote will be 'Go on!' "

NAMES

John means "Jehovah has been gracious"

Howland in English means "someone who lives near a hill"

William is German for "resolute protector"

Bradford is Anglo-Saxon for "broad ford"

"He sent from above,
He took me; He drew
me out of many waters."
Psalm 18:16

HISTORY

The Pilgrim group began in a town in northern
England. They made a simple living on small farms. The
people wanted more religious freedom than King James
and the Church of England would allow. Some chose to
stay in the church and purify it. They named themselves
Puritans. Some chose to leave and hold their own meetings. They were called Separatists, but both were
Pilgrims. "[They] were hunted and persecuted on every
side so as their former afflictions were as flea-bitings in
comparison of these which now came upon them. For some were taken and clapped
up in prison, others had their houses beset and watched night and day . . ." wrote

William Bradford in the journal he kept for twenty years
while he served as governor of Plymouth Colony.

"Yet this was not all, for though they could not stay . . .
the ports and havens were shut against them," he continued. They left secretly after many troubles, and arrived in
Amsterdam, Holland. They were not used to a large city
and soon moved to the town of Leyden, where they lived for
twelve years and worked mostly in cloth-making trades.
Poverty came upon them, so they decided to venture to the
New World because of hardships described in the story. The
group bought the leaky *Speedwell*, but needed more for the
trip. They found several Londoners willing to pay for the
Mayflower and provisions if they would be repaid. Others,
called the Adventurers, joined them sailing only in the
Mayflower on September 6, 1620 from Plymouth, England.
"They knew they were pilgrims . . ." wrote Bradford. That is
how they got the name Pilgrims.

Halfway across the Atlantic a sudden storm hit. A main beam of the *Mayflower* broke and imperiled the ship. The Pilgrims argued about whether to continue their trip, and even the sailors could not agree. They held the beam in place with a heavy jack that the Pilgrims had probably brought for house building. During another storm, John Howland fell overboard. He held onto a topsail halyard rope, sank several fathoms, and was hauled in, according to Governor Bradford's journal.

John survived and did help build Plymouth in the New World. He gained his freedom and had a big family of ten children. He was a Puritan, but his brothers, Arthur and Henry, who joined the colony later were Quakers. Trouble began to brew early for Quakers in the strict Puritan colony.

They tried communal food production, but it failed. They succeeded when each family worked its own plot of land. Look up a Plymouth Plantation map for John Howland's house and plot.

Creative Writing

sand blotter

Check here if you did this in your story.

(tips from the author)

Let your reader see from the main character's eyes, from his or her POINT OF VIEW. For example, from underwater John Howland would see the sailor leaning over the side of the ship as a blurry face. Keep a single point of view. Read your main character's mind, but only his or hers. When you show someone's thoughts, you are showing his or her point of view. You can draw what John saw underwater.

WORD STUDY

Work with a partner. Compare your definition with the dictionary. Check if similar.

1.   Use clues from the story.   2. Use a dictionary.   3. Check

        Fill in with your definition.   Write definition.   ✓

a .   precarious _____   _____   ____

        _____   _____

b.   winch _____   _____   ____

        _____   _____

c.   knickers _____   _____   ____

        _____   _____

d.   draper _____   _____   ____

        _____   _____

QUESTIONS TO DISCUSS

1. What is a primary historical source? Would Governor John Bradford's
    HISTORY OF PLYMOUTH PLANTATION be one? What kind of first hand
    information can you find in a primary source? Find out about their communal
    farming.

2. Considering the pros and cons in the story, would you have chosen to
    sail to America or to stay in Europe? Why?

3. Why do you think John Howland came up from the cabin above the gratings on
    deck? Try to read his mind.

4. Has God gotten you out of a scary situation? Let's PRAY: (You may include
    thanks in your prayer.)

    _____

    _____

    _____

UNIT 4   RUN, ISAAC!

"Is that a rap at the door?" Sarah said softly to her husband. Mr. Macy rose. As the heavy door creaked open, lightning flashed against a black sky and into the cabin. It was a cold and stormy night in Salisbury, Massachusetts in 1659. Who could be visiting on such a night? Isaac wondered. He stood at the window, but the five young Macy children huddled in the dark corner behind their mother in her rocking chair.

Thomas Macy motioned a welcome. The strange man in a black cloak and broad-brimmed hat hesitated, then stepped into the kitchen. Raindrops falling from his cloak made puddles on the braided rug. Thunder crackled.

Mrs. Macy prepared a place for the man at the table. "Here, eat," she said as she ladled chowder from the kettle into a bowl. The man eased himself into a chair. The aroma of codfish and biscuits wafted through the room.

"I thank thee, Mrs. Macy. Many miles have I trod through the forest." The man leaned his elbows on the table, supporting his head in his hands. Light from the huge stone fireplace flickered on his rugged features. "Puritans have banished Quakers. They want to drive us away. The Boston sheriff is close on my heels. He will chain me in jail if he finds me," continued the man, "and thee, too, Thomas Macy, for helping me."

The man's words sent a chill up Isaac's spine. Isaac turned to Mr. Macy. Mr. Macy chained in a dungeon!

Thomas Macy was not Isaac's real father. Isaac was alone in the world when he was ten, but Mr. Macy had taken him in to do farm chores. He had given Isaac a

23

place to stay, but now Isaac longed to be a real part of the family. He wished Mr. Macy would think of him as a son.

The Quaker ate the last of his biscuit as the storm let up. "I thank thee, Goodman Thomas," said the Quaker. He wrapped a piece of Mrs. Macy's blueberry cobbler for his cloak pocket. He left, disappearing into the dark willows along the river.

Several days passed. Late one afternoon, Isaac delivered a sack of flour to the Salisbury Inn, putting it in the root cellar as usual. He turned to leave and heard someone upstairs say "Macy." Hiding in the shadows, Isaac edged up the ladder under an open trap door to listen.

"Word has it that Thomas Macy sheltered a Quaker during the frightful storm," snarled a husky man. "He must pay for this crime, and we plan to catch him!"

Crash! The sack fell from Isaac's trembling hands and broke, spattering flour on the dirt floor. The trap door slammed shut. Isaac scurried down the ladder. He careened out the cellar door.

He had to warn Mr. Macy. Stumbling and falling over rocks and roots, he ran as he never had before. He ignored the cuts and pain.

Panting, he flung open the cabin's front door. "Mr. Macy, they're coming to get you . . . five big men! They . . ." Isaac sank into the closest chair and stammered as he told the rest of what he had heard.

Mr. Macy paled. "This is it! Sarah, our plan! Signal the neighbors!"

Sarah opened the front door and struck the cowbell. Beads of sweat glistened on his brow as Mr. Macy pried a stone from the hearth. He pulled out a parchment and held it up. "A map to Nantucket. They call it the Far Away Island. Natives live there, no Puritans. If we can cross the sea, we might be safe."

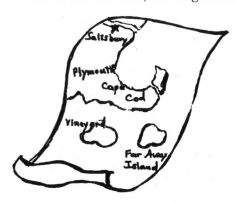

They rushed to pack a few clothes and pieces of bread into blankets, which they tied at the corners. Isaac remembered the blueberry cobbler Mrs. Macy had baked the day before. He turned back to get it.

24

When Isaac reached the front door with the cobbler, the Macys were well ahead of him. In the orange sunset they made a procession of silhouettes as they quickly descended to the river's edge. He could see in the dimness their two neighbors by the water.

Isaac's heart sank. He couldn't bear it if they left without him. He clutched the dish and dashed for the river. He waded in as the boat swung from the shore. Mr. Macy grabbed Isaac's outstretched hand and pulled him in.

Sarah settled the children down into the hull with the few bundles. "Be still," she whispered. Dusk began to fall.

At once, Mr. Macy took the oars and rowed with firm, quiet strokes, his jaw set. No one spoke. The boat glided in the darkness down the Merrimack River.

Isaac's heart raced. There was no time to think of the house they'd left by the weeping willows. He listened for crackling branches to warn them of the sheriff's men, but heard only the dripping of water from the oars.

Soon the smell of sea air gave Isaac hope. On the open ocean they could be safe.

"Unfurl the sail!" Mr. Macy drew in the oars and gripped the tiller at the stern. Waves began to rock the boat.

Mr. Starbuck and James from upriver fumbled in the dark with the ropes. At last the sail puffed out, catching a breeze that blew south. Isaac watched the sparkle on the tips of the waves. He hoped no one on shore could see them in the moonlight. They sailed all night.

At sunup they rounded Cape Cod. "The sky!" One of the children pointed. "Look at those black clouds!"

"Winds from the northeast!" called Mr. Macy.

Isaac felt a chill as waves broke in little spurts and then big splashes over the bow.

"Lash the oars!" shouted Mr. Macy, struggling to hold the tiller and steady the boat. The adults held the children in a tight circle. Could Isaac tie the precious oars to keep them from washing overboard? He must!

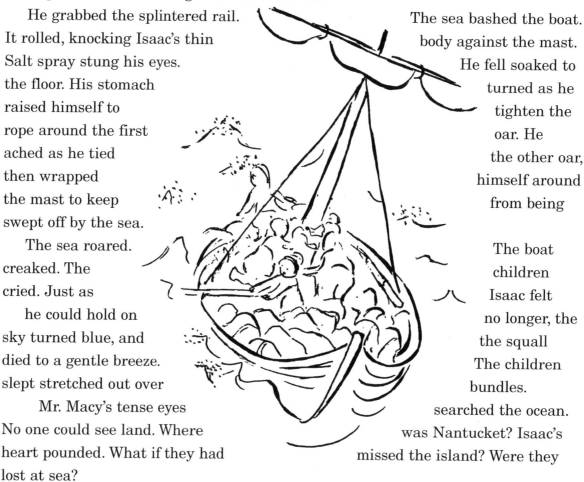

He grabbed the splintered rail.   The sea bashed the boat.
It rolled, knocking Isaac's thin   body against the mast.
Salt spray stung his eyes.   He fell soaked to
the floor. His stomach   turned as he
raised himself to   tighten the
rope around the first   oar. He
ached as he tied   the other oar,
then wrapped   himself around
the mast to keep   from being
swept off by the sea.

The sea roared.   The boat
creaked. The   children
cried. Just as   Isaac felt
he could hold on   no longer, the
sky turned blue, and   the squall
died to a gentle breeze.   The children
slept stretched out over   bundles.

Mr. Macy's tense eyes   searched the ocean.
No one could see land. Where   was Nantucket? Isaac's
heart pounded. What if they had   missed the island? Were they
lost at sea?

Isaac scrambled between the children and bundles to the narrow bow.

He wedged himself in at the front to see farther. The boat sailed on. He waited, sometimes dozing off. At last, he spotted a sliver of gray in the distance. Was it what he hoped? It began to rise above the ocean.

"Land ho!" he called. The sliver gradually became a sandy shore as they approached. It turned green with shrubs and wigwams. Mr. Macy wrestled their boat through rough surf onto the shore. The children jumped out and skipped up the beach.

With the boat hauled in, Mr. Macy took Isaac aside. "Son," he said, putting his

arm around Isaac's shoulder,
and a swift runner.
with news of danger,
    Son! Isaac
smiled. They
Isaac had a

"You are a worthy sailor
    Because you ran so fast
we are now all free."
    looked up at him and
would all be safe, and
family to call his own.

NAMES

Isaac
means "laughter" in Hebrew

Thomas
is Irish for "tall as a tower"

Sarah
means "princess"

Tristram
means "din, son of thunder"
in old Welsh

Edward
is "guardian of property"
in Anglo-Saxon

Starbuck
could be from shepherds
who put a star on their
prize buck goat

27

HISTORY

J G Whittier

John Greenleaf Whittier wrote in his poem,
"The Exiles," about Macy. (paraphrased)

As the rain began to fall,
a stranger bent and sore,
From fleeing through the forest
Could run and walk no more.
He knocked upon the farmer's door.

"Friend, will you shelter me?"
The hopeful stranger whispered
"Though it may endanger you
To help one such as me
Who seeks what'ere is true."

Thomas Macy was summoned in 1659 to appear before the Puritan
Massachusetts Bay Colony court. Instead of appearing he told the court that he
would tell the truth, that on a rainy day four men asked him to direct them to
Hampton [New Hampshire] . . . He thought they might be Quakers. The time they
stayed in the house was only three-quarters of an hour. . . . He had not willingly
offended.

In the meantime Thomas was building an open boat and making plans to flee to
Nantucket Island. He, along with a man by the name of Tristram Coffin and sever-

al others, bought parts of the island for thirty pounds
sterling and two beaver hats. The Puritans did not
relent and Thomas paid a fine.

Nevertheless, he decided to take his chances with Native Americans on Nantucket. The people in the story took the boat from the Massachusetts Bay Colony, probably through a Cape Cod canal, out into the ocean. They discussed ways to protect themselves once they arrived, as there were about three thousand Natives on Nantucket. Knowing that they were afraid of the mentally infirm, Edward Starbuck agreed to act like a crazy person if they were hostile. A sudden squall arose, but Thomas guided the boat to Nantucket. Natives there did befriend them, sharing dried corn and venison from their underground caches, or holes lined with stones.

Several years later the Natives did a powwow dance near Thomas's house. Edward thought they were about to attack Thomas and his family, so Edward came running, flailing his cane over his head, acting as wild and crazy as he could and calling on God for help. (Psalm 91) Sachem, chief Nickanoose, must have respected that because he and Edward Starbuck became good friends. Edward learned the Algonquian language so he could communicate better with his Native American friends.

Creative Writing

Check if you did this in your story.

(tips from the author)

Show your main character's hopes and dreams by what he or she does. Isaac hoped to become a real part of his new family by running swiftly with news of danger. Circle or underline parts of Isaac's story that show other things he did to feel important in the family.

WORD STUDY

Look up the following words and write each one in a sentence.

willow _____

hearth _____

cobbler (as in story) _____

peril _____

silhouette _____

sterling _____

QUESTIONS TO DISCUSS

1. What were some of Isaac's feelings throughout the story?

2. Whom did the Puritan Massachusetts Bay Colony's intolerance affect? How?

3. Look at Mr. Macy's boat. What boats were in the Bible? How did God use them? Look at the shape of the mast and crossbar. What does that represent? How do both of these symbols relate to each other? Let's PRAY:

_____

_____

_____

You may
draw a picture
of a boat
in the
Bible.

"They that dwell
in the wilderness
shall bow before him."
Psalm 72:9a

UNIT 5

SAMSON'S WIGWAM

A One Act Play

(Settings are described by narrator)
(Props can be imaginary)

SAMSON OCCOM (young)

SAMSON OCCOM (adult)

DANIEL (colonial boy)

LITTLE WOLF (Native American)

REV. WHEELOCK (teacher)

JOSHUA RUNNING BROOK (teenager)

DAVID SINGING BEAR (teenager)

SMILING TURTLE (child)

JULIA WHITE DOVE (child)

other children

extras optional

NATHANIEL WHITAKER (friend)

WAITER or WAITRESS (English)

LORD DARTMOUTH (English)

PALACE GUARD (English)

NARRATOR

SCENE 1

TIME: July, 1733

SETTING: Outdoors at the town of Mohegan in eastern Connecticut

NARRATOR: The year is 1733. Our story opens in the village of Mohegan in the American Colony called Connecticut. There we meet Samson Occom and his friends, Little Wolf and Daniel. (*two Native American children right*)

(*Two Native American children (right stage) work on a cat's cradle. Samson and a colonial boy are looking at a book (center stage).*)

LITTLE WOLF: Samson, come join us. You make the best cat's cradle. (*Children tangle string & get frustrated.*)

SAMSON: I am busy with a talking book. Make the book talk again, Daniel.

DANIEL: "But the path of the just is as the shining light, that shineth more and more unto the perfect day." (Proverbs 4:18)

SAMSON: Where can I get a talking book?

DANIEL: Here, your name means "the sun," so you take it. (*hands Samson the book*)

SAMSON: Thank you, Daniel. Will you teach me to speak from the talking book?

DANIEL: I must help my father plow the bean field, but I know someone who can teach you.

SAMSON: Who is it?

DANIEL: You will have to walk ten miles through the forest. Follow Beaver Creek upstream to the fork. Pass to the right by the foothills. At the waterfall is the cabin of Reverend Wheelock.

(*Samson and Daniel wave and leave in opposite directions. Little Wolf and his friend shake their heads at the string and exit.*)

SCENE 2

NARRATOR: Three years later at Rev. Wheelock's cabin school

REV. WHEELOCK: It is time for a friendly game of recitation.

Mohawks on my right versus Mohegans on my left. The losing team must haul firewood for the winning team during the next week. Whoever can finish this line of poetry gets a point. Ready? "Live . . . I will . . ." Sam Occom.

SAMSON OCCOM: "And dwell as in my center, as I can." by Mr. Ben Johnson.

REV. WHEELOCK: One point for the Mohegans. "A merry heart" Joshua Running Brook.

JOSHUA RUNNING BROOK: ". . doeth good like a medicine." the book of Proverbs. (17:22)

REV. WHEELOCK: One point for the Mohawks. "The quality of mercy is not strained," David Singing Bear.

DAVID SINGING BEAR: "It droppeth as the gentle rain from heaven . . ." by Mr. William Shakespeare.

REV. WHEELOCK: Two points for the Mohegans.

NARRATOR: The Mohawks won that game, and Samson did go on to get an education. He studied English, Greek, Hebrew, mathematics, and history. Then seeing such great need, he went out to start his own school for Native American children.

SCENE 3

SETTING: Samson and his young students sit in front of his wigwam surrounded by corn plants. Motions are pantomimed with imaginary plants or brown paper plants.

NARRATOR: It is now September a year later at Montauk, Long Island. Samson is teaching students at his wigwam school, but Samson's school is poor. He has no books, so he has made cedar chips with a letter on each.

33

SAMSON: Who can spell "corn"? (*He holds a "birch bark" construction paper container with "cedar chip" adhesive-backed notes, each marked with a letter.*)

(*Some children raise hands.*)

SAMSON: Smiling Turtle.

SMILING TURTLE: (*She comes up, picks letters, and sticks letters to brown paper panel held up*) K-O-R-N.

SAMSON: Almost.

(*Some children raise hands . . .*)

SAMSON: Julia White Dove.

JULIA WHITE DOVE: (*Comes up and spells*) C-O-R-N (*on panel*)

SAMSON: Good. (gets thoughtful and strokes his chin) You know, when you children grow up, you will need a college to go to so you can know the ways of the English. There is no college for Indians now. Someday I want to start one. If only I had the money. Maybe my friend, Nathaniel Whitaker, and I will go to England to ask for help. Maybe we will even see the queen? (*waves his hand*) Oh, that is only a dream! Lesson is over for today. It is time to go to the field, children, and I must work for my customers.

(*Children go to the sides of the stage to "weed" the corn. Samson covers a book.*)

CHILD 1: This corn is so dry . . . Look how it tips over. This stalk is bent in half.

(*Each child pulls up a corn plant and brings it over to show Samson.*)

CHILD 2: (*shakes the plant next to Samson*) Look how dry and sandy this is!
CHILD 3: (*holds his plant up*) This one falls apart.

CHILD 4: And mine has no ears! (*looks at the plant*)

CHILD 5: We won't have corn for syrup corn pudding!

CHILD 6:	We are hungry now!
JULIA WHITE DOVE:	(*dashes up to Samson bringing a "birch-bark" white construction paper container decorated with flowers drawn in magic marker to look like beadwork, she holds it out to him*) Here, Mr. Occom, take this gift to the queen. I made it myself.
SAMSON:	I will, Julia White Dove. (*He wipes a tear from his eye.*)
NARRATOR:	Samson talked with Rev. Wheelock, who liked the idea of a Native American college. He helped Samson and Nathaniel Whitaker prepare for their voyage to England. John Hancock, a rich businessman from Boston, gave them money toward the boat trip.

SCENE 4

NARRATOR:	It is 1767 in a London pub. For months, Samson has spoken all over England at churches and meeting houses about his hopes for a Native American college.
WAITER OR WAITRESS:	(*pours tea for Samson and Nathaniel*)
NATHANIEL:	(*sips tea and looks at the clock, he is agitated*) Lord Dartmouth should be here with our invitation to the queen's birthday. It is getting late.
SAMSON:	I will present Julia White Dove's basket to the queen and then tell about our hopes to build a college for Indian young people.
NATHANIEL:	You can practice while we wait, Samson. (*puts two chairs in front of the table facing them to the side*) Here, think of the king and queen on their thrones. Now, present your gift (*motions with arm*).
SAMSON:	(*holds basket in front*) I must curt? curt? (*curtsies awkwardly*)
NATHANIEL:	Curtsey? No. That is for ladies.
SAMSON:	The queen is a lady.

NATHANIEL:	Ladies curtsey. Men bow. Here, let me show you. (*stands to Samson's side so audience can see Samson, shows him how to bow*)
SAMSON:	(*bows awkwardly, then better as he practices two or three times*) Dear Queen Charlotte (as he bows)
NATHANIEL:	No, no, no (*shakes his pointing hand*) Your *Majesty*, Queen Charlotte
SAMSON:	Your *Majesty*, Queen Charlotte (*he bows*) — a gift from my student, Julia White Dove. (*sets basket on table*) Your Majesty, King George, in 1616 your ancestors, King James the First and Queen Anne received Pocahontas, daughter of Chief Wahunsonacawh. She, whom the English renamed Rebecca, brought much food to the starving Jamestown Colony.
NATHANIEL:	She was most helpful to the English. (*nods*)
SAMSON:	Later, Squanto of the Wampanoags, taught the hungry people of Plymouth how to grow corn.
NATHANIEL:	It was a good thing for them. (*nods*)
SAMSON:	And Sachem Nickanoose gave food to the English on the Far Away Island, Nantucket, so they could survive the winter.
NATHANIEL:	They might not have lived. (*shakes head*)
SAMSON:	But your English settlers have taken land where we used to grow corn and even more land where we hunted for game. Now my people, the Mohegans, cannot grow good corn or find wild game. We are hungry. (*pause*) If my brothers and sisters will live with the English, they must learn their ways. We hope to build a college for Native youth.
LORD DARTMOUTH:	(*dashes in holding the invitation in the air*) I have it — the invitation to Queen Charlotte's birthday!

NATHANIEL: Is it too late, Lord Dartmouth?

LORD DARTMOUTH: Our horse lost a shoe. We had to wait for the smithy. (*English accent*)

NATHANIEL: Quickly! Quickly!

(*They hurriedly gather up their gifts and follow Lord Dartmouth out the door.*)

SCENE 5

SETTING: The front door of the palace and a guard stands near it, in front of a pile of books

NARRATOR: A short time later in front of the palace (*Lord Dartmouth, holding out the invitation, Samson, and Nathaniel come up to the guard, all FACE the audience.*)

LORD DARTMOUTH: (*Holds out the letter*) Our invitation to the queen's birthday! (*English accent*)

GUARD: So sorry, sir. Her majesty and the king just left. You are too late. (*English accent*)

LORD DARTMOUTH: (*turns to Samson*) Oh, Samson, (*in a disappointed voice*) now you cannot tell the queen about the Indian college.

GUARD: Ah, yes, the Indian college. (*turns to the stack of books behind him and takes a third of the books*) The queen directed me to give these to Mr. Samson Occom, Mohegan.

SAMSON: (*steps forward*) I am Samson Occom, Mohegan. (*takes books*)

LORD DARTMOUTH: (*turns to Samson*) The queen must have heard about your speeches.

GUARD: (*hands a third of the books to Lord Dartmouth and a third to Nathaniel*)

SAMSON: (*bows to the guard and straightens*) Please thank your
                          Queen Charlotte and King George for the books. We are
                          most grateful.
(*Samson, Lord Dartmouth, and Nathaniel leave with the books.*)

NATHANIEL: (*mutters to Samson, but so audience can HEAR*) You *only*
                          bow to the king . . and queen!

THE END

NAMES

Samson (Samson)
in Hebrew is "the sun"

Occom
refers to "on the other side"

Nathaniel
is "God has given" in Hebrew

Whitaker
means "white acre," "small plot
of land," or "part of the cemetery
for the poorest" in English

HISTORY

Samson Occom, a Mohegan Native American, grew up hunting and fishing with his father. He could not read or write. At the age of twenty, he went to Rev. Wheelock's school for Native Americans. He spent four years there and learned English, Latin, and Hebrew. He started his own wigwam school for native children in Montauk, Long Island. He put letters on cedar chips in order to teach his students to read.

Samson

Samson became an ordained minister. He conducted Sabbath and Wednesday services in his wigwam. He taught and preached with enthusiasm. He used colorful, figurative speech in English and his native language. Many Native Americans became Christians during the Great Awakening of the early 1700s. Mary, his wife, was a partner in his missionary work. Samson felt hurt that white missionaries received larger salaries. He had to hunt, fish, work in wood, and cover books with deerskin to provide enough food for his family.

Later, Samson and Nathaniel Whitaker, with help from John Hancock, traveled to England to raise money for a Native American college. Samson preached to large gatherings all over Gr. Britain and raised money for the college. Lord Dartmouth took Samson to meet King George III as he prepared for Parliament. Samson wrote in his diary that, as he watched the king put on his diamond-studded crown, he thought about how a heavenly crown so outshines the earthly crown. Samson did get to see the festival of the queen's birthday, and the king did give him books for the college, which became Dartmouth College in New Hampshire.

Nathaniel

CREATIVE WRITING

(tips from the author)

Show feelings of the main character. Samson felt frustrated in trying to help his people. He wiped a tear from his eye. Pretend you are the director of the play. Write into the script some stage directions telling your actors how you want them to move in order to show Samson's feelings. You may draw some figures and facial expressions.

Draw the pen back in the ink-well if you did this in your play or story.

WORD STUDY

The way these words look to you might have been the way English first looked to Samson. Unscramble the following words to fill in the blanks.

chemsa   notuCcentic   usyrp   ysturce   gaMohen

1.   Native Americans sweetened their food with maple _____

2.   Samson was a _____.

3.   A _____ is a leader of Native Americans.

4.   _____ is south of Massachusetts.

5.   It is customary for a woman to _____ to royalty.

QUESTIONS TO DISCUSS

1.   Why did Samson tell his students they needed to learn the Englishmen's ways?

2.   Discuss the meanings of the four quotes in the play.

3.   The white man took much land from Native Americans. Are there ways Native Americans can be treated more fairly today? What is it like to live on an Indian reservation? Let's PRAY:

_____

_____

_____

Blessed is the nation
whose God is the LORD,
and the people whom He
hath chosen for His own
inheritance. Psalm 33:12

UNIT 6

WHO WAS BEN FRANKLIN?

Scientist?

Inventor?

Speaker?

Tinkerer?

Organizer?

Jokester?

Statesman?

"TART WORDS MAKE NO FRIENDS: a spoonful of honey will catch more flies than a gallon of vinegar."

Seven-year-old Ben blew his shiny new whistle all over the big household, disturbing everyone. He boasted of how he had spent his own coppers. But his many brothers, sisters, and cousins told him he had overpaid. In his own words, Ben remembered, "They laughed at me so much for my folly, that I cried with vexation."

"DO FOR THE FUTURE"

At sixteen Ben resolved "to do for the future all that lies in my way for the service of my countryman." In his autobiography he writes, "So few were the readers at that time in Philadelphia, and the majority so poor . . . I proposed that we should bring our books to [a] room, each of us being at liberty to borrow . . ."

Ben Franklin thought about what people needed to improve their lives. He helped bring communities together to start public libraries, volunteer fire departments, and insurance systems.

"HIDE NOT YOUR TALENTS, they for Use were made. What's a Sun-Dial in the Shade!"

Ben Franklin tinkered with gadgets to make colonial life more convenient. He made a chair that turned into a step ladder. He created a device which he called an "arm," that took books from a high shelf. He improved home heating and ventilating systems. He wanted to share his ideas with the new country.

Throughout American history, Native Americans often said that the English spoke with forked or double tongue, when the English failed to live up to their treaties.

Ben Franklin's grandfather, Peter Folger, learned the Algonquian language where he lived on Nantucket Island. Peter preached Christianity to Native Americans there, and he often mediated situations between the English and Native Americans.

One such situation occurred in 1665. The native chieftain, King Philip (sometimes natives took English names), came with his men in war canoes from the mainland. He came to catch a Nantucket native, who had spoken the name of Philip's father, Massasoit. According to Native American rule there, speaking the name of a high-ranking member, who had died, was punishable by death.

King Philip's warriors captured Jonathan Gibbs, the object of their pursuit, and were planning to kill him.

Can we as bystanders be still and not speak, to let Jonathan die? Peter wrote to the affect afterwards.

The English then told the chief they would gather together people of the island and attack him if he did not let Jonathan go. There were only thirty-five English men and boys who could be summoned to fight. Peter's and Edward Starbuck's sachem friends did not side with King Philip, so King Philip took a payment and left.

Ben Franklin spoke of his grandfather's writing as having "decent plainness and manly freedom."

Later in Ben's own life, he was summoned to mediate between Native Americans and a colonial mob. He reasoned with the mob that if a Native American hurts me, should I then hurt every Native American I meet? Or if a redhead hurts me, after that should I attack all redheads? The mob thought about it and dispersed.

IN GOD WE TRUST

"WITHOUT JUSTICE COURAGE IS WEAK"

Benjamin Franklin was a former slaveholder, but later in his life he acknowledged that slavery was wrong. He became president of the Pennsylvania Society for Promoting the Abolition of Slavery. In 1789 the Society urged Congress to use every power to discourage traffic in the persons of our fellow man.

For free African-Americans he helped found a school to teach trades.

President John Adams said that Ben took lightning down out of the sky and sceptres away from tyrants.

Franklin studied the little considered force of electricity, bringing to it the idea of positive and negative charges. He developed lightning rods to protect houses during thunderstorms.

He contributed to bringing America freedom from England. In England, he argued for representation, and in France he helped get support for the Revolutionary War. In the Declaration of Independence, Ben agreed with "We hold these Truths to be self-evident, that all Men are created equal, that they are endowed by their Creator with certain Unalienable Rights." Ben was the only person to sign all four documents: the Declaration of Independence, the treaty with France, the peace treaty with Great Britain, and the United States Constitution.

The Great Seal of the United States makes a print on official documents such as treaties. The print can be seen on the one dollar bill. Before the Revolution, Ben Franklin, Thomas Jefferson, and John Adams proposed the eye of Providence to symbolize the new country's hope for divine favor. Franklin had also suggested a scene of Pharaoh and his army chasing the Israelites through the Red Sea, Moses at the head guided by a pillar of fire and cloud. After the Revolution, for the opening of the Constitutional Convention, Benjamin suggested there be prayer. Speaking to George Washington, he asked why had they not called upon the "Father of lights" before? He continued that if God notices a sparrow fall, then an empire could not rise without His help.

IN GOD WE TRUST

"HASTE MAKES WASTE"

English merchants complained that east to west travel across the Atlantic Ocean was slower than west to east. In his trips across the Atlantic, Ben had become aware of the Gulf Stream by doing experiments. He asked a cousin, Timothy Folger, who was a whaleman, to chart the Gulf Stream from Mexico to England. Timothy did and Benjamin published it, advising that the west-bound ships avoid it. The British, however, continued to complain about their slow route for years and did not listen to the "know-nothing Americans" who made good time with it.

Mark Twain said that his grand-father knew Ben Franklin. He says that if someone came upon Ben unexpectedly when he was catching flies, or making mud pies, or sliding on a cellar-door, he would immediate-ly toss out a maxim, and walk off with his nose in the air and his cap turned around, trying to appear wise and eccentric.

45

"DILIGENCE IS THE MOTHER OF GOOD-LUCK"

Ben wrote to his mother, Abiah Folger Franklin, Philadelphia, April 12, 1750.
"As to your Grandchildren, Will is now 19 Years of Age a tall, proper Youth, and much of a Beau. He acquir'd a Habit of Idleness on the Expedition, but begins of late to apply himself to Business . . .

Sally (Sarah) grows a fine Girl, and is extremely industrious with her Needle, and delights in her book. She is of a most affectionate Temper . . . She goes to the Dancing School."

NAMES

Benjamin

is "son of my right hand" in Hebrew

Franklin

means "freeholder" in English and German

Abiah Folger, Peter Folger's daughter, moved from Nantucket to Boston where she married a widower, Josiah Franklin. Josiah had seven children from his first wife. Then he and Abiah had ten more. Benjamin was the youngest son.

Benjamin performed a wide range of civic and political activities during the colonies' struggle for independence, so he could be called a "right hand man." "Freeholder" is an appropriate meaning for his last name, because he worked so hard for freedom from England.

Among his friends were George Washington, Thomas Jefferson, and John Adams. He knew presidents, kings, queens, and lawmakers, as well as shopkeepers and farmers.

Creative Writing

(tips from the author)
Research facts in which you think your readers would be interested. Most people know about Ben Franklin's lightning rod, so I described the "arm" for books, Gulf Stream study, and lending libraries in America. Circle or underline three particularly interesting new facts you learned about Ben Franklin.

Draw the pen in the ink-well if you did this.

My MAXIM

_____ _____

_____

_____

Almanack

folly _____

resolve _____

insurance _____

_____

tyrant _____

summon _____

disperse _____

abolition _____

sceptre _____

autobiography _____

_____

QUESTIONS TO DISCUSS

1. What were 5 things Benjamin Franklin did for freedom?

2. What were 5 things Benjamin Franklin did to improve everyday colonial life?

3. What would your maxim be? You may illustrate it.

4. What do you think Ben may have said to King George III and the British Parliament to persuade them to repeal taxes on the colonies?

5. How can our country today "look to the LORD"? Let's PRAY:

_____

_____

King James I had the Latin Bible translated into English, so common people could read it.

   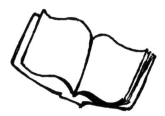

King James Version

Founding Fathers read the Bible

"For the LORD is our judge,   **the LORD is our lawgiver,**   **the LORD is our king;**   **He will save us."**
Isaiah 33:22

JUDICIAL
Branch

interprets laws
according to the
Constitution;
CANNOT make laws,
policy, or add to
the Constitution

LEGISLATIVE
Branch

representatives
of the people
make laws;
individual's
rights to his or
her own life,
liberty, and
property are to
be respected

EXECUTIVE
Branch

enforces laws as
guided by the
Constitution,
can encourage
legislation and veto
(George Washington did not want
the president to
be like the king.)

Checks & Balances

Judges and Courts   Senate and
House of Representatives
(Both are the Congress)

President

49

The Founding Fathers believed in

LIMITED GOVERNMENT

Before the Revolutionary War, American
Colonists complained about **too high
taxes**, such as the Stamp Tax and the
Tea Tax. In 1773 Bostonians threw British tea overboard in the Boston Tea Party,
so they would not have to pay the tax.

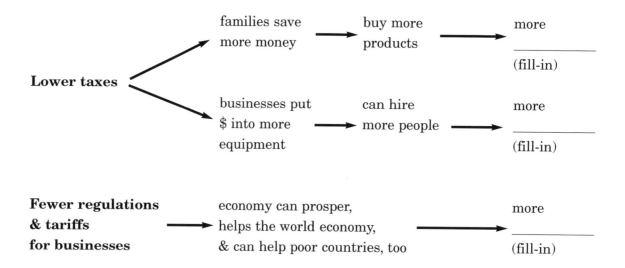

Lower taxes

families save
more money → buy more
products → more
_____
(fill-in)

businesses put
$ into more
equipment → can hire
more people → more
_____
(fill-in)

**Fewer regulations
& tariffs
for businesses** → economy can prosper,
helps the world economy,
& can help poor countries, too → more
_____
(fill-in)

UNIT 7   GEORGE WASHINGTON SAW THE HELP OF PROVIDENCE

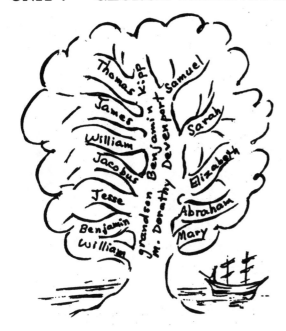

Jacobas Kipp sailed
from Holland in 1632
and married Maria de
la Montaune in the
Dutch fort, New Neth-
erlands, now New York.

"And the LORD went before them
by day in a pillar of a cloud
to lead them the way, and by
night in a pillar of fire to
give them light, to go by day
and night." Exodus 13:21

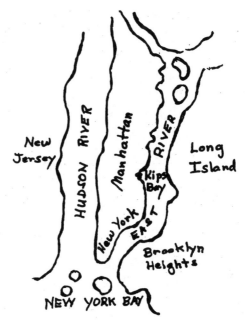

George Washington camped with the Continental Army at Brooklyn Heights, Long Island, in August 1776. Thousands of British and Hessian soldiers surrounded the Americans. Many British ships waited in New York Harbor blocking their escape. But sailors from Marblehead, Massachusetts were gathering their small boats secretly on the East River. They wrapped their oars with cloth.

The sailors began, on August 29, to ferry soldiers across the East River to Manhattan as the sun set. The evening was stormy and progress slow, but at midnight the waters became calm. Then the sailors rowed back and forth fast, finishing safely under a thick fog at dawn.

The British, stunned over the escape, crossed the East River and invaded at Kips Bay, but the Americans retreated north. The Continental Army was saved.

More help from **Providence**

Squanto, a Patuxet Native American who knew English, helped the Pilgrims survive. He interpreted between the Pilgrims and Native Americans for a treaty that lasted fifty years.

The French Navy sailed to attack the east coast of the colonies in 1746. On October 16, New England held a day of fasting and prayer. That night a storm dispersed the French fleet and prevented the attack.

Cornwallis's British Army pursued the Continental Army throughout 1782, but storm swollen rivers more than once blocked them, while the Americans escaped.

Reread the Preface page about Providence and discuss.

Creative Writing Idea

You may choose a character in one of these events—a sailor, a soldier, George Washington, a citizen—and write a story from his or her POINT OF VIEW. Describe sounds, sights, smells, and weather conditions. Include your main character's emotions and thoughts, especially about help from Providence.

_____   _____
character   **event**

"And the Spirit of God moved
upon the face of the waters."
Gen. 1:2b

UNIT 8
LETTER TO A SON

When Benjamin Coffin Starbuck, a captain of a merchant ship, stopped in Peru, in October 1846, he wrote from Lima to his son, George Fred. Benjamin came from a long line of whaling men and had himself been captain of a whaling ship before sailing a merchant ship. Edward Starbuck, who had sailed out to Nantucket with Thomas Macy and Isaac, predicted that his children's children would fish the sea for a living.

Settlers began hunting whales off the shore of Nantucket in the 1600s. Their ships became larger as they traveled farther and farther, until they did much of their whaling in the Pacific Ocean. Sometimes their trips would take two to four years. Nantucket became the whaling capital. Whale oil lit lamps around the world, and whalebone was made into accessories for women's fashion.

clipper ship

Often seamen turned to the merchant trade. Clipper ships, with their sleek hulls and many sails, carried goods across oceans with the greatest speed ever of all sailing ships until that time.

Captain Starbuck sailed south from Nantucket, then through the howling Straits of Magellan or around the Horn of South America. He would stop in Chile or Peru, then cross the Pacific to China. He took on cargoes of silks or pearl shells. One time his ship met a terrible typhoon on the coast of China. He wrote in his log that they "set down the light spars," but even so every sail was split. A large hole sprung in the ship. They had two pumps working and were able to cover the hole with two sheets of copper. Later they rigged their spare set of sails.

VICTORIA HALL

To
Geo. F. Starbuck.

My dear son.

Having —

— now a leisure moment, and thinking you
have arr'd at an age, in which you can understand
what I write; I will employ this moment, in laying
before you a few principles of your duty, both to God, & Man.
My Dear Child, God has given to you, and to all
men Talents. By the prudent and persevering, who
not only use but improve them, every thing really
desirable may always be attained; but without industry
no natural gift can possibly avail them; you must
seek with humility and diligence for God's blessing on your
endeavours, and his direction in all your pursuits, but
remember it is foolish and presumptuous to expect
success even in a good cause otherwise than
appointed; and it is his will that we attain all
real advantages, both for this world and that which is
to come, by earnestly endeavouring to obtain them by
vigilance. The advantages of a good character and a
clear conscience are well worth your utmost efforts.
Ever preserve, a humble confidence in Heaven, and a
pious observance of religious duties, and then your virtue
will strengthen with your years. Be humble in prosperity,
firm in adversity, suffer not the smiles of man to
divert you from the service of God; resist every incitement
to dissipation, every temptation to luxury; Should you
ever become rich & happy, surrounded by splendour, friends
& fortune, let it lead you to think on the many helpless people
who languish in poverty, and eat the the bitter bread of
affliction, moistened by their tears; and seek to remove the

54

misery and may one day share, but which, whether you partake or not, it is your express duty to relieve. And learn that in the sorest trials comfort and support may be derived from faith and prayer; poverty relieved by industry and patience; and comfort expected from unforeseen sources, since our Heavenly Father never fails to send help to his Children— in the hour of need.

... as I shall have ... time, ...
I am your beloved Father,

Benj: E Starbuck

Give my love to your good Kind Mother, in whom I trust you place implicit confidence, and render ... obedience in all things. Strive to do all the good you can for her, and love her, and your heavenly Father will register it in heaven.

Lima Oct 11th /46

Reprinted by permission:
Nantucket Historical
Association,
Starbuck family papers,
MS 144 folder 49;
www.nha.org
to research library
to Barney geol. ecds.

You may imagine
you are on a
whaler or clipper
ship and
write to your family
back on Nantucket.
  (page 58)

My dear son.

George Fred Starbuck

My dear son,

During now a leisure moment, and thinking you have arrived at an age, in which you can understand what I write; I will employ this moment in laying before you a few principles of your duty, both to God, & Man.

My Dear Child, God has given to you, and to all men Talents; By the prudent and persevering, who not only use but improve them, everything really desirable may always be attained; but without industry no natural talent gift can possibly avail them; you must seek with humility and diligence for God's blessing on your endeavors and his direction on all your pursuits, yet remember it is foolish and pre-sumptuous to expect success even in a good cause otherwise* . . . appointed; and it is his will that one attain all real advantages, both for this world and that which is to come, by earnestly endeavoring to obtain them by Vigilence.

The advantage of good character and a clear conscience are well worth your utmost efforts. Ever preserve, a humble confidence in Heaven, and a pious obser-vance of religious duties, and then your virtue will strengthen with your years.

Be humble in prosperity, firm in adversity, suffer not smiles of man to divert you from the service of God; Resist every invitement to dissipation, every Temptation to luxury.

Should you ever become rich and Happy surrounded by splendor, friends, & for-tune, let it lead you to think on the many helpless people who languish in poverty, and eat the bitter bread of affliction, moistened by their tears; and seek to remove the misery you may one day share, but which, whether you partake or not, it is your express duty to relieve.

And learn that in the severest trials comfort and support may be derived from faith and prayers; poverty relieved by industry and patience; and comfort expected from unforseen sources, since our Heavenly Father never fails to send his help to his Children—in the hour of need.

It will not be long ere I will have you with me.

I am your beloved father.

Benjamin Coffin Starbuck

Draw the pen
back in the
inkwell when
you finish your
letter.

Give my love to your good
kind mother, in whom I trust
you place explicit confidence,
and render . . . obedience in all
things, Strive to do all the
good you can for her, and love
her and your heavenly father
will register it in heaven.

Lima   Oct. 11, [18]46

*What do you think Benjamin
wrote that would make sense?
Maybe you can get clues by
thinking carefully about what
he wrote before and after this line?

_____

_____

_____

You may write your own letter.

Geo F Starbuck

"If the Son therefore shall make you free, ye shall be free indeed."
John 8:36

UNIT 9

A LITTLE LADY
A One Act Play

LUCRETIA COFFIN (young)

LUCRETIA COFFIN MOTT (adult)

JAMES MOTT (her husband)

MOTT children: ANNA
                     MARIA
                     ELIZABETH
                     THOMAS
                     MARTHA

FRIEND LAURA

JAILER

JUDGE KANE

BAILIFF

LAWYER FOR SLAVES:
   THADDEUS STEVENS

THREE SLAVES:
   WILLIAM BROWN
   MILLER THOMPSON
   SAMUEL HANSON

THREE WHITE DEFENDANTS:
   CASTNER HANAWAY
   ELIJAH LEWIS
   JOSEPH SCARLETT

PROSECUTOR: JOHN ASHMEAD

58

SCENE 1

NARRATOR: On Nantucket Island, over twenty miles out in the ocean from Cape Cod, lives the Coffin family. It is the year 1800 and seven-year-old Lucretia is writing a letter to her father at sea. (*seagull sounds on tape — if possible*)

LUCRETIA: (*as she writes*) To Captain Thomas Coffin, TheWhaler T R Y A L (*spells out*), Pacific Ocean. Dear Father, (*as she thinks about what to write, she looks down at her bright, blue bows, she raises one foot to admire it*) I hope thy ship is good and thou hast "greasy luck." How many whales didst thou catch? (*looks at bows again*)

Baby Mary runs a lot now. I have to tend her when Mother opens her shop in the front room. Mother is teaching me to

Tape a copy of the letter to the desk — for a prompter, use an imaginary inkwell.
Be sure the waste-basket does NOT block view of bows.

stitch my sampler. I am up to "H." (*looks at both bows to admire*) We go to meeting every Sunday. Friends talk about being simple, "plain living" they call it. I got some blue bows from Rachael. She's not a Quaker. Thinkest thou I shouldst keep them? Maybe I will not. I really do like them. Friends at meeting say we should be simple and help people in trouble. I want to be a good Quaker. (*takes imaginary scissors out of her desk, pantomimes cutting off bows as she detaches taped on bows, and throws them into a wastebasket*)

Please finish thy whales and come home soon.

Hugs and kisses.   Love, Lucretia

NARRATOR: Lucretia loved her Nantucket Island, but when she was eleven, her family moved to Boston, and she went away to boarding school. Though she missed the Island, she threw herself into her studies. By the time of her graduation she had fallen in love with a tall, quiet young Quaker named James Mott. Soon they were married.

SCENE 2

TIME: 1851 (for the purpose of the skit)

SETTING:	The Mott's dining room in Philadelphia. James and Lucretia are at each end of the table. The children are along the backside.
NARRATOR:	The Mott's dining room in Philadelphia, 1851.
LUCRETIA:	Finish thy beans, Elizabeth, so thou mayst take a sweet. (*These are imaginary sweets; eating—pantomime.*)
ELIZABETH:	(*"gobbles up" imaginary beans*)
LUCRETIA:	That's good, Elizabeth. Now thou mayst take a sweet. (*hands Elizabeth plate of "sweets," children — EXCITED*)
ELIZABETH:	(*takes a "sweet," passes plate to Anna, unwraps her "sweet," "eats" it, slowly makes a face—"tastes" badly*)
ANNA:	(*takes plate, takes a "sweet," passes plate to Martha, "eats" it, slowly makes a face because it "tastes" badly*)
MARTHA:	(*repeat, passing plate to Thomas*)
THOMAS:	(*repeat*) Mother, this is not sweet.
LUCRETIA:	But children, these candies are made by free labor, and thou hast a verse with thy treat. Anna, which verse hast thee?
ANNA:	"Do not be afraid of this to eat. No slave hath worked to make this sweet."
JAMES:	Children, thy mother is right. When we use slave-grown products, we encourage slavery.
THOMAS:	But Father, thou sellest cotton from the South.

JAMES: It troubles me. We make a good living now, and I don't know if I could do as well selling Pennsylvania wool. I have eight mouths to feed.

LUCRETIA: James, dear, we must think of the slaves toiling in the hot sun.

JAMES: Well, then, if thou and the children canst live on it, then we will sell Pennsylvania wool—no slave-grown cotton.

LUCRETIA: And Martha, what is thy verse?

MARTHA: "Am I not a woman and a sister?"   (actual quote)

(*An urgent knock at the door interrupts.*)

THOMAS: (*goes to the door*) Who goest there?

FRIEND LAURA: Friend Laura.

THOMAS: (*opens the door*) Welcome.

FRIEND LAURA: Thank you, Thomas. (*rushes over to Lucretia*) Lucretia, there has been a slave rebellion in Christiana and several slaves are in prison.

LUCRETIA: We must go visit them to see what we can do. (*grabs her shawl by the door and turns toward the table*)

JAMES: (nods) All right, dear.

LUCRETIA: Children, help thy father with the dishes. (*Lucretia and Laura go out.*)

SCENE 3
TIME: November, 1851.

SETTING: Two adjoining cells in a Philadelphia prison. Three whites in one cell rub their hands before an imaginary heater, three fugitives in the other cell—no heater—they shiver. Jailer sits in front at center, slouches with his arms crossed.

61

NARRATOR:	The Fugitive Slave Act, which passed in 1850, stated that a slave owner had the right to recapture his slaves even in northern states. In 1851 in the small town of Christiana, Pennsylvania, several escaping slaves defended themselves against their master's party, which followed them up from the South.
LUCRETIA:	(comes up to the jailer with her friend, FACE audience)
JAILER:	What is a little lady doing in a place like this?
LUCRETIA:	We have come to see the slaves thou hast so unjustly imprisoned.
JAILER:	(rudely) Well, (pause) you have big ideas for a little lady!
LUCRETIA:	(straightens her back, but in a normal tone) We intend to speak with them.
JAILER:	(taken aback, looks surprised, pause . . .) Oh well, what can two little ladies in bonnets do? (laughs as he opens the cell door)
LUCRETIA:	(Lucretia and her friend come into the slaves' cell.) We are Friends. Please tell us thy story.
WILLIAM BROWN:	(cautiously, the two others hold back) My name is William Brown. This is Miller Thompson and Samuel Hanson. We got away from mean old Master Edward. But he came after us. We fought him, and those (points) three white men came to help us. Master is dead now, but his men caught us and brought us here. What will happen to us? We are so cold, Missus, and hungry.
LUCRETIA:	(turns to her friend) We will check the ladies sewing circle.
LAURA:	We shall find something there.
LUCRETIA and LAURA:	(turn to go) We will be back with clothes and bread.

NARRATOR: Lucretia and her friend visited the slaves in the days before the trial.

SCENE 4

NARRATOR: It is three days later in a Philadelphia courtroom. (*Bailiff leads three fugitive slaves, wearing red, white, and blue scarves, and three white prisoners to right side of the judge's bench, as the judge and lawyers come in from the left. Lucretia and her friend follow.*)

LUCRETIA: (*brushes past the judge and says sideways to him, but so the audience CAN HEAR*) Remember the traitor to humankind is the worst kind of traitor.

(*The judge looks surprised at Lucretia as she calmly takes a seat next to the slaves, her friend sits next to her—all seated so the audience can see each one — Lucretia and friend start imaginary knitting motions on red and white mittens, lawyers take places on each side of the room.*) NO KNITTING NEEDLES

BAILIFF: All rise. (*people rise*)

JUDGE: The case of the deceased Mr. Edward Gorsuch's estate versus his fugitive slaves, William Brown, Miller Thompson, and Samuel Hanson, also Mr. Lewis, Mr. Hanaway, and Mr. Scarlett. The slaves are charged with resisting arrest, in which outbreak Mr. Gorsuch died. The white men are charged with refusing to help with the arrest. All this is illegal under the Fugitive Slave Act of 1850 and subject to prosecution. Be seated. (*bangs gavel*) (*This speech can be on desk.*)

LUCRETIA: (*gives the judge a frown as if to say, "Thou knowest it is wrong to hold the slaves. They were just fighting for their freedom."*)

JUDGE: (*comes down from the bench over to Lucretia*) Mrs. Mott, you must not stare at me like that! You are interfering with this trial. You must move your chair. (*points to several feet away, goes*

63

back to bench, she moves chair there) Lawyer for the defense, how do your clients plead?

LAWYER FOR DEFENSE: (*rises*)

LUCRETIA: (*As he speaks, still seated and imaginary knitting, she edges her chair back to where it was.*)

LAWYER FOR DEFENSE: (*while Lucretia is moving*) Not guilty, sir. It was self-defense, your honor, and the three white gentlemen felt it was against their conscience to help with the arrest, that in truth it would be . . . a crime against humanity!

JUDGE: So you are saying you believe this law is wrong?

LAWYER FOR DEFENSE: Yes, your honor, I am.

LUCRETIA: (*gives the judge a "You know he's right" look*)

JUDGE: (*strokes his chin, mumbles — but so audience CAN HEAR*) Remember, the traitor to humankind is the worst kind of traitor. (*shudders and shakes his head*) Oo, I don't want that! You win Mrs. Mott! The case against these three fugitives and three white men is dropped. (*bangs gavel, turns to the fugitives and says loudly*) Go! Quick! Before I come to my senses!

(*All the defendants stand. William comes out and Lucretia meets him center stage.*)

LUCRETIA: (*hands William the mittens which are red and white—symbolic of Canada where he is going—he puts the mittens on so the audience can see. She goes off stage with William, as other fugitives, etc. exit.*)

THE END

NAMES

Lucretia
comes from the Latin word "lux,"
which means "light"

James
is a "follower after"

Quakers
"trembling at the word of
the Lord"

Mot
is French for "word"

Creative Writing

(tips from the author)
Let your audience know what is happening through the
dialogue. For example, Friend Laura tells Lucretia that there
has been a rebellion at Christiana. Circle or underline parts of
the dialogue that tell you what has happened or is happening.

Draw the pen
into the
inkwell if
you did this
in your story
or play.

You may write a letter to a "relative on a ship in the Pacific." Use dialogue to make
it more real.

WORD STUDY

Paraphrase the following. (Say the same thing in your words.)

Free labor _____

_____

. . . thou hast unjustly imprisoned_____

_____

We intend to speak with them. _____

subject to prosecution _____

traitor to humankind _____

HISTORY

Frederick Douglass, an escaped slave who knew Lucretia, said of her, that the speaker wore the usual Quaker dress . . . and brought words of light and love. They both spoke at anti-slavery meetings throughout the country.

Lucretia Mott

Frederick Douglass

Lucretia was born into the large Coffin family on Nantucket Island in 1793. Her father, Thomas, was a whaling captain and away at sea much of her childhood. Her letters to her father would have been taken by ship to the Pacific Ocean and probably dropped into a whale-oil barrel mailbox on the Galápagos Islands. When her father brought his ship there, he could check the mailbox for letters from her.

One of Lucretia's relatives, Mary Coffin Starbuck, years earlier held Quaker meetings in her front parlor and helped spread Quakerism, or the Society of Friends, throughout Nantucket.

Lucretia, as a young child, believed in the Quaker values of simplicity and helping those being treated unjustly.

She may have rebelled somewhat at their customs, but when she grew up, she wore plain Quaker dresses in gray or dark colors with a shawl and bonnet. But she liked color and would make bright carpets for their house.

She married James Mott, a businessman, and was busy raising their six children. As the children grew up, though, she spent more time on her interest in trying to end the injustice of slavery.

Their house was sometimes a stop on the Underground Railroad. A fugitive would fill up on Lucretia's cooking and then relax in their back yard under the shade of James's broad-brimmed hat.

Lucretia said that we must destroy the system of slavery, root and branch. At their home they entertained many abolitionists: Frederick Douglass, a prominent leader; the former slave and speaker who renamed herself Sojourner Truth; people who worked with James at the busy Underground Railroad station where Harriet Tubman brought "passengers"; John Greenleaf Whittier, the antislavery poet; and William Lloyd Garrison, a speaker from Boston.

Harriet herself came to their home to visit Lucretia. Lucretia helped her make connections to other UGRR agents.

She invited so many people to dinner that she and James had a table made that could expand to more than thirty feet long. She served fruits and vegetables that grew in their back yard. Peas grew along the fence. Their guests would discuss issues of the time, especially slavery. After dinner she would bring a tub of soapy water and set it at the end of the table. Guests would pass their plates down the long table and she would wash them there, so she could be a part of the conversation. She had always liked to talk.

According to the memoirs of some guests, she would wave her dishtowel for emphasis.

When Lucretia was not entertaining at home, she traveled throughout the country speaking against slavery, often a dangerous thing to do. She traveled with James or with a lady friend. Sometimes she drove a horse and buggy by herself to meetings. She even spoke in the South.

Scene 4 is based on fact. Lucretia really did glare at the judge, and she did move her chair back after they made her move it. She and her friends knit red, white, and blue scarves for the fugitives.

Lucretia helped organize the Philadelphia Female Anti-Slavery Society with black and white women. She and James helped form the American Anti-Slavery Society. No one thought that men and women could work together in the same group, but Lucretia thought so.

The Motts traveled to England as delegates in 1840 to the World Anti-Slavery Convention. All the women had to sit in a separate section watching and could not join the men in discussions. Lucretia sat next to Elizabeth Cady Stanton. They talked together about how unfair it was that only men could speak at the meeting. Lucretia and Elizabeth, back in America, planned the first women's equality convention in Seneca Falls, New York, in 1848.

Lucretia, growing up on Nantucket Island, had seen women managing businesses while their husbands were away on long voyages at sea. Her mother would take their whale oil and candles to trade in Boston for household goods like cloth to sell in her front parlor store. Lucretia, more than many mainland women, thought men and women were equal. Later on Susan B. Anthony joined Lucretia, Elizabeth, and other women in the struggle for equality. Susan worked mostly for women's right to VOTE.

QUESTIONS TO DISCUSS

1.   What character traits did Lucretia's mother need to manage while her husband was at sea?

2.   How were Lucretia and James, her husband, trying to discourage slavery?

3.   What were the unfair conditions in the jail?

4.   Why do you think the judge dismissed the case and released the fugitives?

5.   What do you think Lucretia might have said at gatherings in the South?

6.   What are some ways we can help prevent slavery around the world? (Some Christian charities help people in very poor countries start small businesses.)

Let's PRAY:

_____

_____

_____

"Thou shalt not
deliver unto his master
the servant who
has escaped from his
master unto thee."
Deut. 23:15

UNIT 10

LEVI'S LOCOMOTIVE
A One Act Play

LEVI COFFIN (young)

MR. COFFIN (father)

LEVI COFFIN (adult)

CATHARINE COFFIN (wife)

SLAVEDRIVER

SIX SLAVES (optional)

FOUR COFFIN CHILDREN

SLAVE CHASER

FUGITIVE SLAVES — 3 women, 2 men

BOAT TICKET-TAKER

SAILORS   2

PEOPLE ON SHORE

PEOPLE ON BOAT

NARRATOR

SCENE 1

NARRATOR: Mr. Coffin, a Quaker, chops wood by the side of the road while his seven-year-old son, Levi, watches. It is 1805 in New Garden, North Carolina.

(Six slaves, chained together, come down the road.)

MR. COFFIN: *(pantomimes chopping wood)* Why do they chain thee?

SLAVE: *(with sad expression)* They have taken us away from our wives and children. They chained us so we cannot escape back to them. *("chains" of thick black yarn tied LOOSELY, NO paper)*

SLAVE DRIVER: (harshly) Hush! Move! (waves them on)

YOUNG LEVI: Father, we would feel terrible if someone took thee away. Why did that angry man want to take them?

MR. COFFIN: Levi, there are some men who want to make other men work for no pay. It's called slavery. Some men say they own others, but no man can own another.

YOUNG LEVI: Can they ever escape?

MR. COFFIN: Some try but are beaten if they are caught.

YOUNG LEVI: I will help all the slaves I can to get away from mean people like that man. *(Slaves pass out of sight.)*

MR. COFFIN: Son, thou wilt have to do it without fighting. Remember, thou art a Quaker.

ALTERNATE SCENE 1 *(Slaves NOT played by actors.)*

NARRATOR: same top line plus "Six slaves chained together can be seen down the road."   —skip to—

SLAVE DRIVER: same line by a voice off stage   —continue scene

SCENE 2
TIME: February 1827

SETTING: Levi and his wife, Catharine Coffin, at their dinner table in Newport, Indiana, now Fountain City. They are sipping tea with tired gestures.

NARRATOR: Levi remembered the face of that sad slave for many years. During his growing years, Levi took food to slaves escaping through fields near his house. He married Catharine, a young Quaker. He told her he wanted to do more, and she said, "Let me help." They moved to Newport, Indiana, in 1830.

CATHARINE: Levi, thou hast had a busy day at the store. It is nearly mid-night . . .

(*A soft knock at the door, Levi and Catharine look at each other, Catharine blows out an imaginary candle*) [*LOWER LIGHTS*]

CATHARINE: Who's that?

LEVI: The TRAIN!

(*Catharine looks out the window toward the front door. She nods to Levi. Levi opens it, five fugitives are at the door. They are not dressed for cold weather.*)

FUGITIVE: (*pause*) . . Friend? Can you help us?

LEVI: Come in (*motions with a "sh" signal*).

(*Fugitives act cold, shiver. Catharine quickly pulls down window shades, then peeks out the edge of the window. She leads the fugitives in to sit at the table — flurry of activity.*)

LEVI: (*bolts the door with a large gesture, sits at the table*) From where art thou?

(*Catharine goes to the hearth and serves imaginary soup.*)

73

FUGITIVE:	Way down the Mississippi. We followed the North Star. And Freedom! We're bound for Freedom! No more chains! No more whips! No more master! Master and his dogs chased us!
CATHARINE:	Come . . . eat. It's hot.

(*Children come "downstairs," yawning and rubbing their eyes.*)

CATHARINE:	Children, come, please serve our guests.
LEVI:	(*looks out the window*) Catharine! Quick! The men are here, armed men! Quick! To the hideaway!

(*Catharine helps direct the fugitives to the "stairs"—another door. One child leads them "upstairs," while Catharine and the other children scurry to hide the bowls. Then the children follow "upstairs." Levi and Catharine sit quietly at the table drinking tea. Loud knocks at the door.*)

LEVI:	Who goest there?
SLAVE CHASER:	(*gruff voice*) I want my property!

(*Levi slowly opens the door.*)

SLAVE CHASER:	(*gruff voice*) You must know where my property is! Two men and three women.
LEVI:	Thy property, sir? I do not know where thy property is. Thou shouldst take better care if it, then thou wouldst know where it is.
SLAVE CHASER:	(*goes away mumbling, but so the audience can HEAR*) I'm going to find the tunnel to his underground railroad. I know he's got one!!
LEVI:	(*closes and fastens the door, turns to Catharine*) I did not lie. These fugitives are not his property, for no man can own another. I truly do not know where his property is.

CATHARINE: (*puts her hand on his arm*) Thou hast spoken well, Levi.

LEVI: It is not safe in our garret. Tomorrow night I will go to the barn and "stoke my locomotive" with oats. My "locomotive" and I will take them to the ferry for Canada. That man will be searching for two men and three women. He will NOT look for a fine lady dressed in silk with four porters (*winks at Catharine*).

CATHARINE: The sewing circle has made a fine dress for such an occasion. We have men's clothes, too, Levi.

SCENE 3
[*FULL LIGHTS*]

TIME: Morning two days later

SETTING: Two sailors and a ticket-taker are on the deck of the *Lake Erie* ferry. Levi and the fugitives blend into the crowd gathering on shore by the gangplank. On the dock a "chain" holds the gangplank. Seagulls and lapping waves (*on tape if possible*) (*chain as in scene 1*).

TICKET-TAKER: (*on the ferry by the gangplank*) All ABO-A-R-D the *Lake Erie* . . . Next stop, CANADA.

(*Two or three passengers board the gangplank. Fugitive dressed as "Miss Emily" steps up to the gangplank just as the slave-chaser comes to stand in front of her. He pauses to look at her, steps back, and watches her.*)

"MISS EMILY": (*wearing a hat, veil—see-through enough so she can walk—and long gloves, flounces skirt as she sashays up the gangplank, turns to look back, her four "porters" follow bumping into each other with the bags to create a distraction*) Watch that bag, John! (*not too politely*)

"JOHN": Yes, Miss Emily.

"MISS EMILY": Joe, don't be clumsy!

"JOE": No, ma'am.

75

TICKET-TAKER: Move! Move! Move!

"MISS EMILY":   Hurry up, George!

"GEORGE":   Coming, Miss Emily.

"MISS EMILY":   (*hands in her ticket*) These are my four porters. (*turns around*) Careful with those packages, tsk, I say.

(*Two or three more passengers board. The fugitives gather at the rail to look at the crowd on shore.*)

TICKET-TAKER: Gangway! (*sound of "boat" horn, NOT too loud*)

(*Two sailors lift the chain, as if heavy, and pile on <u>shore</u> side.*) (*This is symbolic of the chains of slavery they are leaving.*)

LEVI: (*surreptitiously touches the brim of his hat and nods slightly to those bound for freedom*)

(*The group of escaping slaves waves, and the crowd on shore waves back.*)

SCENE 4
TIME: 1870

SETTING: Podium at the front of a hall in Cincinnati, Ohio, behind it is a semicircle of chairs. Catharine, the Coffin children, and others are seated there.

LEVI: (*enters wearing his broad-brimmed hat and comes up to podium with written speech*) President Lincoln signed the Emancipation Proclamation abolishing slavery in 1863. The cannons of war fell silent in 1865. Now we are here on this great day in 1870 to celebrate the signing of the 15th Amendment to the Constitution that gives all men the right to vote, whatever their color.

For thirty years I was called the President of the Underground Railroad. The title was given to me by slave-hunters who could not find their fugitive slaves after the slaves came to my safe house. Many of the fugitives came from Alabama, Mississippi, Louisiana, from all parts of the South. The number of fugitives that I aided was several thousand, but not one so far as I know was captured and taken back to slavery. Providence seemed to favor our efforts for the slaves and crowned them with success. They found freedom on the "train." But the business is done, the "stock" has gone down, and the "railroad" is "rusty." (*takes off his hat and sets it on the podium*) I resign my post on the Underground Railroad. (*turns and walks away from the podium, leaving the hat*)

NAMES

Levi in Hebrew is "one who serves in the temple"

Catharine means "pure" in Greek

Coffin means a "small basket"

HISTORY

The Underground Railroad was busy during the sixty years before the Civil War. It may have received its name from men that chased slaves who seemed to vanish, as if taking an underground railroad. In reality, the Underground Railroad was a network of stations, or "safe" houses, located about twenty to thirty miles apart from the South reaching up to Canada. A few others were named "president" in various centers of the UGRR.

When slaves considered running away, a conductor might teach them a song that would give them directions to a northern state. One such song was "Follow the Drinking Gourd." Runaways looked to the sky and followed the Big Dipper, or Drinking Gourd. The front of the dipper points to the North Star. If clouds covered the stars, fugitives would feel the trees for moss. That side would be the northern exposure, and so they could continue.

Fugitives usually traveled at night with or without a conductor. They fled on foot, took boats, sometimes even a train, and carts. Levi's cart had a false bottom to hide people.

"And the LORD spoke unto Moses, "Go unto Pharaoh, and say unto him, 'Thus saith the LORD: Let My people go, that they may serve Me.' " " Exodus 8:1

Harriet Tubman was probably the most famous conductor on the UGRR. Moses, as she was called, herself escaped from slavery,

Harriet Tubman

then returned to the South many times, risking her own life to lead many people to freedom. She said the Lord guided her.

At each station a fugitive would be given directions to the next stop and told the "safe" signal as he or she started out.

A light in an upstairs window often signaled a safe house. When all was clear, one stationmaster hung on the clothes-line a quilt designed with a house and smoking chimney.

Inside a safe house, fugitives would be hidden during the day. A pile of potatoes or coal might have a "room" inside. Levi and Catharine hid runaways in a space under the eaves and pushed their bed over the entry.

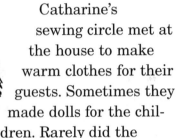

Catharine's sewing circle met at the house to make warm clothes for their guests. Sometimes they made dolls for the children. Rarely did the women know if someone was hidden upstairs.

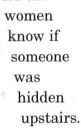

Levi faced opposition for many years, sometimes from other Quakers. Most ministers for a long time even in the North justified slavery with their religious views. Levi was threatened by pro-slavery people and sometimes pelted with rotten vegetables or worse; but he continued to help people who were being abused, as did his cousin Lucretia.

Levi said what he did he believed was simply his Christian duty.

Creative Writing

(tips from the author)
Keep your reader guessing about how the story or play will turn
out until the very end. The fugitive chaser appeared again in
the play. At the boat dock he almost recognized the fugitives,
but they narrowly escaped. You may * suspenseful parts.

Draw the pen
in inkwell
if you did
this in your
play or story.

WORD STUDY

Draw a line from each word in List A to its matching word in List B.

List A	**List B**
gesture	fireplace
fugitive	swagger
hearth	rude
gruff	motion
sashay	runaway

QUESTIONS TO DISCUSS

1. What was Levi's Locomotive? What clues helped you find out?

2. Why did the fugitive chasers think Levi had an underground railroad?

3 What were some of Levi's character traits that helped him do what he did?
   Catharine's traits?

4. Even after slavery was abolished in northern states, those states for years
   supported slavery in the south. Why do you think they did? Who was responsi-
   ble for slavery? (The **National Underground Railroad Freedom Center** is
   in Cincinnati, Ohio.)

5. What are "stocks"? Can "interest" have two meanings? Are both meanings
   appropriate for the UGRR? If so, how?

6. If you ran an UGRR station, what would your "safe" signal be? You may draw it.

7. How can you pray for people around the world who are in slavery?
   Let's PRAY:

"And we have known and believed the love
that God hath for us. God is love,
and he that dwelleth in love dwelleth in God, and God in him."
I John 4:16

UNIT 11   **A WARM COAT FOR ANN?**

Great Aunt Ann Whitaker Meserve, born in 1859 in Chatham, New Hampshire, wrote about her life as a pioneer there. She wrote about farming and family, but did not mention school-ing. Perhaps that is why she wrote without punctuation.

when I was nine years old I found I was an
artist my greatgrandmother was sitting in her
little reed rocker and when in a thoughtfull
mood would sit with her finger on her nose
I caught the idea of making her picture
I got my pencil and paper and drew her
picture after that I was drawing pictures
of every thing I could think of one day we
had company I drew a picture of the man horse

"Great-grandmother, please don't rock!"

"Whatever for, child?" Great-grandmother looked over her spectacles at Ann.

"I am drawing you."

"Well, Ann, I did not know you could draw."

"I can't when you keep rocking."

"All right, dear, no rocking." Great-grandmother turned to the book in her lap. "Look at this. The farmer's almanac says we will get an early frost."

"Aayuh," Grandfather answered from his long chair. "That's what my bones say."

"And a hard winter," added Great-grandmother.

"Ssh, now I am drawing your mouth," pleaded Ann. Ann had short brown braids fastened with thick red yarn. She had freckles and hazel eyes that searched for things to draw. She drew everything when she wasn't weeding crops. She drew flowers, trees, and field mice. She drew on sacks, burlap, and brown package paper. She stuck her drawings to walls, doorposts, and window frames of her grandfather's house.

He told her they made the house more happy. He liked to look at her pictures from his place on the long chair,

where day after day he lay sick. Great-grandmother had sent for the doctor.

in the fall my grandfather was sick and he had some beans ready to harvest and he was worring because it was quite cold he expected the frost to come and kill them so I thought to myself I can pull them but I knew he would think I could not as there was half an acre of them so I went out of my own accord and pulled every one I saved the beans and he was glad I think for I did not get a scolding.

82

One day Grandfather stirred from his chair. "My bones say the frost will come tonight. The bush beans won't last," he said.

Ann had seen the pantry and was sure they needed the beans for the winter. "I can bring the crop in, Grandfather," Ann said as she struggled into her worn-out coat.

"Ann, I declare, you look like the cornfield scarecrow!" exclaimed Great-grandmother. "How ever will you keep warm in that?"

Ann rushed through the door. She carried a stack of bushel baskets from the shed out into the bean field. The sun cast a dim light on her work as she darted from one bush to another. After filling some baskets, she stood to catch her breath.

She looked up at the gray clouds that blew in from the northeast. They were tinged with yellow-green. Ann knew this might be a nor'easter. A damp chill pressed the air and crept up her too short sleeves.

A snowflake fell, another, and another until they descended in abundance. Gentle snow began swaying to and fro. Ann dashed from one bush to the next, yanking and plopping them into baskets. She dragged each basket into the root cellar. When she came in for the last time, sprinkled with snow, she had pulled the last plant. Grandfather smiled from his long chair.

Ann hung her coat on a peg by the door and settled into the nearest chair.

"I declare, child," Great-grandmother turned to Ann. "Look at your pitiful coat. You have split a seam!"

The wind grew. Each gust rattled windows that were loose in their frames. Shutters banged against their anchors. Ann shivered. She tugged a quilt from the closet.

"Here is a quilt, Grandpa," she said as she wrapped him in it. Great-grandmother served him a bowl of hot turnip-potato soup.

Ann gathered a heavy, woolen sweater around her shoulders and leaned against the window with her own bowl of soup. She worried about Grandfather as she watched the storm grow. No one could get through, not even the doctor. The snow swirled up, spun around, and swooped back. A raspberry bush danced like a wild man. Ann thought of the little field mice she had drawn and wondered if they were warm in their burrows. She thought of other animals out in the storm.

"Grandpa, tell me a wolf story." She edged a stool next to his chair.

"Long ago when I was a young man," began Grandfather, "many animals roamed the forest. There were mountain lions, bear, lynx, wildcats . . . and wolves. I had been hunting deer one day, hour after hour searching the forest. The sun began to set when I noticed two shiny eyes that stared from the trees, then four, six, and a dozen . . a short howl, then a long one, till there was howling all around. I began to run."

The wind howled as it whipped past the corner of the house. Ann pretended it was the wolves chasing Grandfather.

"I ran as fast as I could muster. The howling got closer. I had to do something. Without missing a step, I tore off my coat and left it lying in the path for the wolves to fight over, dashed into the cabin, and bolted the door."

"Whew! I'm glad you can run so fast!" Ann gave Grandfather a hug.

"Time to go to bed, Ann," called Great-grandmother from the kitchen. Veils of snow billowed down the road. Blizzard! The wind blew into the night as Ann fell asleep, dreaming of wild animals in the woods.

In the morning all lay still and bright. Ann rushed to the window. Could this be the same place that was so fierce the day before? Deep snow covered the bean field. She thought proudly of the bushels safe in the root cellar.

Ann grabbed her coat and snowshoes and began to climb out the window, since the doors were always snowed in by a nor'easter. "Ann!" Great-grandmother called. "You can't go out in that coat!"

Ann, with her head in her hands, sighed and stared out the window. She remembered her walks down the road to Sarah's house. She would look over her shoulder as she went, so she could see the snow-covered Mt. Washington rise higher and higher. She wanted to look at the snow in the trees to see the tiny bits of color sparkle. She wanted to make snow angels with her friend.

"Are you sure I can't go out, Great-grandmother? I'm tired of looking out this wiggly window," complained Ann.

"No, Ann," said Great-grandma firmly, "your coat is not warm!"

Then in the distance, Ann spied the top of the huge rolling barrel drawn by horses. It packed down the snow.

"Here comes the barrel!" she announced. She just made out the tall hat of a man on horseback behind the barrel. She knew that hat. She did a jig around Grandfather's long chair. "It's the doctor! He's coming, Grandfather. He'll make you better and you can get up."

"All right, Ann, you may go out to help the doctor shovel out the front door, but that is all," insisted Great-grandmother.

Before Ann knew it, she and the doctor were through the door. "What is this, an artist's gallery?" The doctor turned to Grandfather. "Who drew these pictures?"

"I did!" called Ann from the hearth.

"I would like to have a picture like these," declared the doctor. "Miss Ann, if you can draw my horse at the hitching post, I will pay you in enough wool for a coat. But, here, put on my coat while you are outside."

Ann snatched her drawing paper, board, and pencil. There she stood before the horse in the oversized coat, its hem buried in snow.

"Hold still, Jethro. I'm drawing you."

The horse stared back at Ann and continued to chew from his feed bag. Nevertheless, soon Ann had her drawing and ran inside.

"You will be fine, Mr. Whitaker, if you take this medicine," the doctor told her grandfather.

She kissed her grandfather on the forehead.

The doctor gave her several coins.

The next day Great-grandmother and Ann traveled on the freshly packed road to the country store. Her braids sprang as she leaped from the wagon. Inside, Ann looked up at the bolts of brightly colored cloth on the shelves.

"May I have the red wool plaid, enough for a coat?" she asked. "And black buttons, too!" The clerk cut the cloth and wrapped it in mounds of brown paper.

At home, Ann spread out on the package paper, while Great-grandmother traced her pattern.

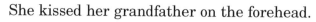

"This is better than
making snow angels, Great-grandmother!"
"Now you will have a warm   winter coat," sighed
Great-grandmother.
"And I will sew on the   buttons!" declared Ann.

NAME

Ann
means "favored" in Hebrew

HISTORY

This story is a composite of two. Great Aunt Ann wrote how she drew a picture of a man's horse when she was a young girl, and the man gave her a new dress. She also wrote about how she raised turkeys and sold them to buy cloth, which a seamstress made for her into a winter dress and coat.

Creative Writing

Draw the pen in the inkwell if you did this in your story or play.

(tips from the author)

Bring in all the senses to your story. Describe sights with color, sounds, scents, and textures. The turnip-potato soup brought a scent into the cabin. I remember, as a child, the wind howling around the corner of our sunroom during blizzards and wanted my readers to "hear" it. Underline sentences about color in red, sentences about sound in green, scents in blue, and texture in yellow. Is it colorful? Try this with your story. Do you need more of a certain color?

WORD STUDY   Make a crossword puzzle or your own study.

QUESTIONS TO DISCUSS

1.   How did you feel when you were trying to read Aunt Ann's writing
      without punctuation or capital letters?

2.   List the ways the characters helped each other.

3.   What did Ann like about the snow?

4.   Ann helped herself by using a talent. What special talents do you have?

5.   How do you think God can use your talents? Let's PRAY:

_____

_____

MY TALENTS   HOW TO USE FOR **GOD**

_____   _____

_____   _____

You may   Dear LORD JESUS, I know I am a sinner and that
pray this   You died for me. I am truly sorry and confess and
prayer: repent. I give You my life and heart and want to
                 live for You. Please use my talents.

Here is **a drawing about my best talents.**

BIBLIOGRAPHY

Unit 1   CHOOSE A NAME

1.   Foster, Marshall, and Mary-Elaine Swanson. *The American Covenant: The Untold Story.* Thousand Oaks, CA: The Foundation for Christian Self-Government, 1981.

Unit 2   POCAHONTAS RENAMED REBECCA

1.   Barbour, Philip. *Pocahontas And Her World.* Boston: Houghton Mifflin Company, 1917.

2.   Benton, William, publ., *Annals of America 1607-1614.* Chicago: Encyclopedia Britannica Inc., 1968.

3.   Cooke, John Esten. *Virginia: A History of the People.* New York: Houghton Mifflin Co., 1896.

4.   Holler, Anne. *North American Indians of Achievement.* New York: Chelsea House, 1993.

5.   Josephy, Alvin. *500 Nations.* New York: Alfred A. Knopf, 1994.

6.   Niles, Blair. *The James.* New York: Farrar and Rinehart, Inc., 1939.

7.   Woodward, Grace Steele. *Pocahontas.* Norman, OK: University of Oklahoma Press, 1969.

Unit 3   HANG ON!

1.   Morison, Samuel. *Of Plymouth Plantation 1620-1647.* William Bradford, ed., New York: Alfred A. Knopf, 1952.

2.   Howland, William. *The Howlands In America.* Detroit: York Press Co., 1939.

3.   Richards, Norman. *The Story of the Mayflower Compact.* Chicago: Children's Press, 1967.

Unit 4   RUN, ISAAC!

1.   Bell, N. S. *Pathways of the Puritans.* Framingham, MA: Old America Co. Publishers, 1930.

2.   Blanchard, Dorothy. *Nantucket Landfall.* New York: Dodd, Mead, and Co., 1956.

3.   Philbrick, Nathaniel. *Away Off Shore.* Nantucket: Mill Hill Press, 1994.

4.   Whittier, John Greenleaf. *The Complete Poetical Works of John Greenleaf Whittier.* Boston, MA: Houghton, Mifflin and Co., 1892.

Unit 5   SAMSON'S WIGWAM

1.   Bible (King James Version). Proverbs 18 and 22.

2.   Clark, George L. *A History of Connecticut.* New York: G. P. Putnam's Sons, 1914.

3.   Hebel, J. William and Hoyt, H. Hudson. *Poetry of the English Renaissance 1509-1660.* New York: F. S. Crofts and Co., 1934.

4.   Love, W: DeLoss. *Samson Occom and the Christian Indians of New England.* Boston: The Pilgrim Press, 1899.

5.   Richardson, Leon B., ed. *An Indian Preacher in England.* Hanover, NH: Dartmouth College Publications, 1933.

6.   Waldman, Carl. *Who Was Who in Native American History.* New York: Facts on File, 1990.

7.   "Whitaker Family" pamphlet, Dartmouth College Archives Library.

Unit 6   WHO WAS BEN FRANKLIN?

1. Cohen, I. Bernard. *Benjamin Franklin: His Contribution to the American Tradition*. NY: The BobbsMerrill Co., Inc., 1953.

2. Franklin, Benjamin, J.A. Leo Lemay and P. M. Zall, ed. *Benjamin Franklin's Autobiography*. NY: W.W. Norton Co., 1986.

3. Franklin, Benjamin, and Richard Saunders, Philom. *Poor Richard: The Almanacks for the Years 1733-1758*. NY: Bonanza Books.

4. Philbrick, Nathaniel. *Away Off Shore*. Nantucket: Mill Hill Press, 1994.

5. Sanford, Charles L., ed. *Benjamin Franklin and the American Character*. Boston: D. C. Heath and Co., 1955.

6. Van Doren, Carl. *Benjamin Franklin*. New York: Penguin Books, 1938.

Unit 7   GEORGE WASHINGTON SAW THE HELP OF PROVIDENCE

1. Foster, Marshall and Mary-Elaine Swanson. *The American Coventant: The Untold Story*. Thousands Oaks, CA: Foundation for Christian Self-Government, 1981; and Mayflower Institute, 1983.

Unit 9   A LITTLE LADY

1. Bacon, Margaret Hope. *Valient Friend: The Life of Lucretia Mott*. New York: Walker and Co., 1980.

2. Bradford, Sarah. *Harriet Tubman: The Moses of Her People*. Kensington, 1989.

3. Bryant, Jennifer. *Lucretia Mott: A Guiding Light*. Grand Rapids, MI: Eerdmans, 1996.

4. Cromwell, O. *Lucretia Mott*. Cambridge, MA: Harvard University Press, 1958.

5. Larson, Kate Clifford. *Bound for the Promised Land: Harriet Tubman*. New York: Random House, 2004.

6. Perry, Roger. *The Galápagos Islands*. New York: Dodd, Mead, and Co., 1972.

7. Sterling, Dorothy. *Lucretia Mott: Gentle Warrior*. New York: Doubleday and Co., 1964.

Unit 10   LEVI'S LOCOMOTIVE

1. Bial, Raymond. *The Underground Railroad*. Boston: Houghton Mifflin Co., 1995.

2. Coffin, Levi. *Reminiscenses of Levi Coffin*. Ben Richmond, ed. Richmond, IN: Friends United Press, 1876, 1991.

3. Petry, Ann. *Harriet Tubman*. New York: Harper Trophy, 1983.

4. Silverman, Kenneth. *The Life and Times of Cotton Mather*. New York: Harper and Row Publishers, 1970.